THE WINGS OF DRACULA

An audio/zoom play by David MacDowell Blue

Based on the novel Dracula by Bram Stoker

© 2021 All Rights Reserved

ISBN: 9798589746648

To inquire about acquiring rights to perform this work
please contact www.offthewallplays.com

CAST OF CHARACTERS
4 women, 4 men, 1 indeterminate

Lucy Westenra (*twenties, female*) Orphaned lady of property and position, engaged to Arthur Holmwood, mistress of Hillingham House, dying of consumption and as a result, fearless.

Mina Murray (*twenties, female*) Schoolteacher, long time friend of Lucy Westenra, engaged to Jonathan Harker. Young for her position, adopts an imperious, even prim manner but feels, passionately. Genuinely religious.

Ellen Renfield (*female, twenties to fifties*) Clairvoyant, currently a charity patient at Dr. Seward's sanitorium. Formerly a seamstress. Terrified by her own visions.

Kate Reed (*female, twenties*) Attendant at Dr. Seward's sanitorium, as former schoolmate of Lucy and Mina. Kind, but somewhat bitter. Alone in the world so devotes herself to her patients.

Arthur Holmwood (*twenties, male*) Aristocrat, works for the Foreign Office, son of a Viscount, engaged to Lucy. Trying very hard to be a proper gentleman, very much in denial about his fiancee's health.

Quincey Morris (*twenties, male*) Gunslinger, best friend/bodyguard to Arthur. American. A natural killer but with a rigid code. Well-educated. Not a hillbilly.

Dr. Jack Seward (*thirties, male*) Doctor, owns/operates a women's sanitorium, former army officer, once and future friend of Arthur and Quincey. Deeply in love with Lucy. Even more deeply feels alone.

Jonathan Harker (*twenties, male*) Solicitor, engaged to Mina, self-made man from a hard scrabble Yorkshire farm. Iron-willed and courageous, determined now to destroy Count Dracula.

Dracula Vampire, namely a walking ghost who drinks blood. Was an Eastern European Warlord in life. Not human. Genderless. For all intents and purposes an Angel of Death.

SETTING
In and around Whitby, England. Including Hillingham House, Carfax, and Dr. Seward's sanitorium for women.

TIME
The year is 1889.

NOTE
This play is written as an audio or radio program. However, it can be simply performed on live stage with microphones, a foley artist, etc. Alternatively it might well work as a Zoom performance (and may well be performed/shown in two parts). When a stage direction begins with FX: this means what follows is a sound or music effect. In keeping with audio drama conventions, each scene change represents a change in specific location.

"The Vampire Sound" mentioned when one of the undead is present can be achieved by use of a water harp. Of course a production might find something which works better.

THE WINGS OF DRACULA

The premiere production of this play was February 14, 2021 via Zoom, through the auspices of Fierce Backbone Theatre Company in Los Angeles, California, USA. The director was Starina Johnson. The cast was as follows:

Dr. Jack Seward	...	Lucas Alifano
Quincey Morris	...	Holger Moncada Jr.
Arthur Holmwood	...	Peter Pasco
Lucy Westenra	...	Beth Nintzel
Mina Murray	...	Holly Hinton
Ellen Renfield	...	Renee DeBevoise
Kate Reid	...	Alana J. Webster
Jonathan Harker	...	Roshan Mathews
Count Dracula	...	Skylar Silverlake

PRONUNCIATION GUIDE

Azrael = AHZ-ray-ell
Beelzebub = BEEL-zheh-bub
Bistritz = BISS-trits
Buda-pesth = BOO-dah pesh
Demeter = DEH-meh-tur
Draught = draft
Godalming = GOD-alm-ing
Hillingham = HILL-ing-hum

Quatre faces = KAA-tra Fass
Seward = SUE-word
Whitby = WIT-bee

HISTORICAL NOTES

In 1889 (the year after Jack the Ripper ripped), the phonograph used by Seward would cost the equivalent of modern sports car.

Any convent in Romania would almost certainly not be Roman Catholic but Romanian Orthodox.

Blood transfusion in this period consisted of using a syringe to pull the blood out of the veins of the donor then push it into those of the recipient. It hurt a lot more than what we do today.

A private women's sanitorium at this time would cater mostly to middle and upper class women dealing with what we would call post-partum depression, stress, general depression, etc. In many ways such a place helped. Nearly all sanitoria also had charity cases, like Renfield. Among other things it added to their prestige.

Should a production wish to be especially accurate when it comes to accents, the following characters are from the North of England, i.e. Yorkshire and Whitby: Mina, Lucy, Jonathan, Kate, and Renfield. Arthur probably sounds as if he is from London. Quincey is an American from Texas but should not sound even remotely like a cowpoke or hillbilly.

In England lawyers fall into two categories—a barrister (who speaks in court), and a solicitor, such as Jonathan Harker. The latter prepares legal documents. One is required to pass a fairly rigorous test in this period to become an official solicitor, although a degree from college or university was not required.

The Church of England, by far the most common denomination in England at this time, eschewed miracles and holy relics or even things like crucifixes, at least in general. That is an oversimplification but will work.

Russia in 1889 was viewed as a dangerous wild card on the European stage.

Unwed mothers then were viewed as fallen women. No such was considered respectable, and certainly could not be employed as a schoolteacher. It happened, of course, and if it could be covered up, it almost always was.

ACT ONE

Scene 1

> *[Office of Dr. Jack Seward in his*
> *Sanitorium, morning. FX: Ticking of*
> *a small desk clock. Distant sounds—*
> *waves, seagulls, a bell—through*
> *window. Then, a wooden box opened,*
> *followed by the arrangement of*
> *machinery, someone preparing an*
> *early phonograph for recording.]*

SEWARD
[Speaking into a primitive microphone, as into a funnel]
Thursday, eighth of August, 1889. Thor's day indeed. Thunder and lightning
all night, reminding me of Egypt. Not sure whether to be grateful for the lack
of sleep. Patients were, naturally, upset. Cannot blame them, although of
course the weather is quite beyond my control. The charity patients, on the
other hand, seem more...well, patient. Housekeeper said at breakfast a ship
wrecked itself on the beach last night. Hope the crew emerged from their
ordeal unscathed. Plan to spend the day usefully busy, and thus resist
temptation to visit Hillingham House without good reason. Have ordered an
especially strong pot of tea, and when it arrives shall proceed with the work I
have chosen for my life. Yes. Work.

> *[FX: Moving again the instruments of*
> *his phonograph, ending with closing its*
> *wooden box.]*

Scene 2

> *[Whitby Beach, morning, continuous.*
> *Enter Arthur and Quincey. FX:*
> *Seagulls, waves, sounds of a busy*
> *harbor, including a bell tolling. Two*
> *pairs of footsteps in the sand.]*

ARTHUR
[Speaking over the wind and noise.]
Well, there she is. Even with the tide, don't think she's going anywhere soon.

QUINCEY
[The same]
Okay. How did she get here?

ARTHUR
The winds of last night's storm literally pushed her through the port entrance,
like threading the eye of a needle. I'd like to call it a fine piece of seamanship.
I would, were there anyone on board.

QUINCEY
Her rigging is pretty much intact. So're her sails.

ARTHUR
Swales says his men left everything in place. Most of them could not wait to get off the ship. We need the log.

QUINCEY
I'll get it.

ARTHUR
We both will.

QUINCEY
Don't think so. Look.

ARTHUR
[Seeing some one approaching]
Oh! I see.

QUINCEY
You've got your fiancee and some other girl to talk to.

ARTHUR
That would be Mina Murray, Lucy's best friend. Quite right.

QUINCEY
Is she pretty? The best friend?

ARTHUR
Very. Rather prim. And, engaged.

QUINCEY
Right. You keep them company. Be back.

[FX: Strong steps fade away in the sand, then splash as they get to to the water. Perhaps we hear someone climbing rigging into a beached wooden ship. Two sets of lighter footsteps approach. Still we hear the waves, wind, and seagulls.]

LUCY
[From a distance]
Arthur!

[FX: Footsteps in sand grow louder.]

MINA
Apologies, my lord, but Lucy would insist on coming down to speak with you.

LUCY
His name is Arthur.

ARTHUR

True enough, Miss Murray. It is my father who is a Lord, not myself. But I must echo Miss Murray's concern, beloved.

LUCY

You are both sweet, and dear to my heart, but I shall not spend my days locked up behind walls. Besides, some doctors have said the sea air might even do me good.

ARTHUR

Lucy--

LUCY

[Interrupting]

We saw this ship go aground. Last night. Almost midnight. Storm kept us awake so we watched it all. Like a series of paintings made visible by lightning. Achingly vivid, really.

MINA

Also, quite bizarre.

LUCY

That, too.

ARTHUR

In what way, bizarre?

MINA

Navigating through the harbor entrance like that? Whoever was at the till must be a genius, or a lunatic belonging in Dr. Seward's sanitorium. Probably both.

LUCY

That would be interesting. Jack's establishment serves women patients exclusively. I quite like that idea—a wild woman of the seas, mistress of her ship, daring and fierce. Oh, the name is even appropriate! *Demeter*!

MINA

You know precisely what I mean.

ARTHUR

There's but one human being on board. The Captain. *[Hesitates.]* And he did not survive.

LUCY

Whatever killed him?

ARTHUR

I would rather not say.

LUCY

Tell me anyway.

MINA

He killed himself?

ARTHUR

Presumably. It could hardly have been an accident.

LUCY

Unless there was someone else on board.

ARTHUR

There was not.

LUCY

How do you know? She went aground hours and hours ago. In the middle of the night. How
can we know who, or what, else might have been aboard? Might have made their way off the ship without anyone noticing. You should have heard what people are saying in the streets.

MINA

Superstitious nonsense.

LUCY

They insist a couple of fisherman saw the Angel of Death leave the ship after it hit the beach.
Like a vast, winged shadow lit up from behind by the lightning. Maybe it was true. Someone did die after all.

ARTHUR

Perhaps so. But since I cannot order the arrest of an Angel, of death or any other variety, that question is outside my purview. *[Catches himself.]* Miss Murray, my deepest apologies. I should have asked last night. Any news of your fiancee?

MINA

Not since you last inquired, no.

ARTHUR

Please allow me to make inquiries on your behalf. Where was...
Mr...Harker?... going, if you
don't mind?

MINA

Jonathan Harker, yes. Transylvania. Somewhere called the Borgo Pass near Bistriz. I last heard from him five and a half weeks past.

ARTHUR

Austria-Hungary, right. Shall cable our Consulate in Buda-pesth no later than this afternoon. Drop some hints, mention a few names. He works at Hawkins and Abbot, yes?

MINA

Indeed. His client is one Count Dracula.

ARTHUR

I understand. That may help. How silly of me. Count Dracula, of course. Is he not the
foreigner who...? Lucy?

LUCY

I apologize.

MINA

Lucy! Lean on me!

LUCY

Have exerted myself a little too much, I fear. Silly of me. No, do not panic. I need but rest.

ARTHUR

We will take you back to Hillingham House.

LUCY

No, Arthur. You have tasks you must complete.

ARTHUR

They can wait.

MINA

That seems unlikely. I shall take Lucy back to the street and find a cab. We will be back at Hillingham in less than an hour. You may come by later. After you've done your duty, as well as sent that telegram.

ARTHUR

You are right, of course.

LUCY

Silly man. Always making us talk you into what you know must be done. Sweet, but silly.

MINA

Wasting time. Come, Lucy.

> *[FX: Steps in the sand begin to slowly retreat. Almost immediately another set of steps return from the ship.]*

QUINCEY

No one alive on the ship except rats. And not very many of those. Just the one man, though. Dead. At the wheel.

ARTHUR

Throat cut, I presume? As Swales said?

QUINCEY

Torn out more like. Days ago.

ARTHUR
Someone steered this ship into harbor.

QUINCEY
Someone else. Should be half a dozen men on a ship this size at least. All gone now. Brought back the log, Its in German.

ARTHUR
A bit much to hope it would be French, I suppose. Or Arabic.

QUINCEY
You know who reads German around here.

ARTHUR
Awkward.

QUINCEY
Just sayin' How's Miss Lucy and her friend?

ARTHUR
No worse, at least. There's that to be thankful for.

QUINCEY
You are one goddamn fool.

ARTHUR
No doubt. We head to Jack Seward's Sanitorium, then. And I need to send a telegram on the way. Was there anything in the schooner's hold?

QUINCEY
Bunch of boxes. Swales said they're full of dirt.

> *[FX: Footsteps and their voices fade, leaving only the sound of waves, wind, gulls and the nearby harbor. They fade away.]*

Scene 3
> *[Interior of a patient's room in Dr. Seward's Sanitorium. Renfield enters. FX: Breathing and the rustle of someone in bed. The harbor is far away, heard through a tiny window. Footsteps approaching in the hall outside, echoing on the floor.]*

RENFIELD
For the blood is the life. And for this reason it shall be poured upon the altar. But it is forbidden to eat the blood.

> *[FX: Knock on the door. Key turns in the lock, and the door opens. Footsteps.]*

KATE REED

Good morning, Miss Renfield. Almost afternoon. Have you managed to get some sleep?

RENFIELD

Very little.

KATE REED

Well, at least you managed to eat some food. But you haven't finished your sausages.

RENFIELD

The taste makes me sick. The bread and tea sufficed.

KATE REED

I thought you liked sausages.

RENFIELD

[Disgusted]
These are under-cooked.

KATE REED

I'll have a word with cook, then. Tell you the truth—last night's storm woke me up as well. And I grew up here in Whitby. You get used to storms coming from the sea. Not like last night, though.

RENFIELD

I almost remember that.

KATE REED

Dreams again? Of being buried alive?

RENFIELD

Worse. Like I was a monster, maybe a dragon, circling over the town like some huge black hawk, or owl. People, they looked like mice.

KATE REED

To fly! That sounds amazing.

RENFIELD

But the mice. The people. I wanted to tear into them. Devour them.

> *[FX: Footsteps down the hall. Door opens and enter Seward.]*

SEWARD

Hello, Miss Renfield. I'm told you had trouble sleeping last night? Maybe the weather stirred things up a bit, eh?

KATE REED

Dr. Seward?

SEWARD

Miss Reed?

KATE REED

I was wondering, might Miss Renfield benefit from a few drops of laudanum?
She slept so little last night?

SEWARD

You've been here how long, Miss Reed?

KATE REED

I meant no disrespect, sir.

SEWARD

Of course not, but—how long? Precisely?

KATE REED

Ten months.

SEWARD

Good. Very well. Tell the dispensary to prepare three drops in water. Bring it
to her once she's finished with her lunch.

RENFIELD

I am quite finished, thank you.

SEWARD

You haven't eaten your sausages!

RENFIELD

I cannot eat them. For some reason. The taste...

SEWARD

Oh my. Sleeplessness and a loss of appetite. My deepest condolences. To lose
one's rest and
then have no desire for food—a terrible combination indeed. Miss Reed, by all
means take those sausages away and get Miss Renfield those drops.

KATE REED

Yes, Doctor.

SEWARD

Rest, Miss Renfield. May your sleep be smooth, and dreamless. Quite. Now, I
have been called away so we shall have our usual talk tomorrow rather than
today. Take the extra time to sleep. Until then.

> *[FX: Footsteps head out of the room
> and into the hall. A food tray being
> picked up.]*

KATE REED

Bet I know where he's going.

RENFIELD

Where?

KATE REED
Hillingham House. Big estate near the abbey ruins. That's where the Westenras live. Or, lived.

RENFIELD
I don't really know Whitby.

KATE REED
The Westenras used to be the biggest landowners around here. They've been selling off their land. This sanitorium used to be one of their estates. Lucy, she's the last of them. We were in school together. I'll take these sausages away and bring you those drops.

[FX: Footsteps as she leaves the room and locks the door behind her.]

RENFIELD
Sweet Jesus, my redeemer—have pity on your servant, I beg. Take this vision away. I cannot bear it. I beg of you. Take it away!

[FX: All the sounds fade into silence.]

Scene 4

[A parlor in Hillingham House, later that day. Enter Mina. FX: An audibly different clock in the background. Louder, deeper, more like a grandfather clock.]

MINA
[Reading aloud the same telegram for the tenth time.]
"I write to inform you Mr. Jonathan Harker heading to England. He says you are to be his wife. All blessings. He came here five weeks past. Evidently spent many days alone in woods. Says much that he survived. Asked me to send this telegram, urges you avoid place called Carfax. I pray God for you. Sister Agatha."

[FX: Doors open, as Mina hurriedly folds the telegram. Enter Arthur and Quincey.]

ARTHUR
Miss Murray! So good to see you again. Allow me to introduce my oldest and best friend, as well as sometimes bodyguard, Quincey Morris.

MINA
Good afternoon, Mr. Morris. Welcome to Hillingham House.

QUINCEY
Thank you, Miss Murray. And, for what it is worth, I apologize.

MINA
For what, please?

QUINCEY

Noticed your reaction to my firearm. I know such is not worn in polite company, but as Arthur said, I am his bodyguard.

ARTHUR

Among other things. Where is Lucy?

MINA

In the next room with Dr. Seward. I asked him to come and examine her.

QUINCEY

We know. Just came from the sanitorium.

ARTHUR

Yes. I also went and sent a telegram to our consulate in Buda-pesth. With even the slightest bit of luck we should be hearing about your fiancee in days, maybe sooner.

MINA

Arthur. A question of two if I may? Jonathan was selling one of Lucy's properties to a foreign nobleman. I believe you know the one. Carfax?

ARTHUR

I do indeed.

MINA

Is it dangerous in any way?

ARTHUR

Yes, I suppose so. Why do you ask?

MINA

I began to wonder why anyone would desire to purchase the place. Why hire a solicitor to travel halfway across Europe for the sake of an abandoned ruin? Can anyone even live there?

QUINCEY

Good questions.

[FX: A door swings open. Enter Seward.]

ARTHUR

Jack! Good to see you!

SEWARD

Arthur. Hello, Quincey.

MINA

How is Lucy, Dr. Seward?

SEWARD

Unchanged in any significant degree. The disease remains active. Today was simply a moment of understandable exhaustion. She should not have walked so far.

QUINCEY

So, how long?

ARTHUR

Quince!

SEWARD

Barring any remission, a year. Possibly two. That however remains a best case scenario. A sudden turn for the worse remains very possible.

ARTHUR

Jack, we stopped by the sanitorium looking for you. Need your help in a non-medical manner if you can spare the time. Quincey, if you would?

QUINCEY

Here is the log of the schooner that went aground last night. Damn thing's in German. We just need to get some idea what it says.

SEWARD

Why not ask the crew?

ARTHUR

The whole lot are missing. All save the man we presume to be the Captain. He's dead.

SEWARD

To be brutally frank, Arthur, I have living patients who demand the overwhelming majority of my time.

ARTHUR

Well, we don't need the whole thing translated. Or even transcribed. If you can but give us some idea of what happened--

SEWARD

Quite impossible. I do apologize.

ARTHUR

But don't you have a staff? Those who can take up the slack as it were for a day, perhaps two? Or, half a day?

SEWARD

At the bare minimum I must supervise all treatment for each patient, in number approximately half that of a company of infantry. My first duty must be to them. If either one of you needs medical attention you may call on me at will.

MINA

[Interrupting the very polite argument.]
Give me the log. I speak and read fluent German.

ARTHUR
Miss Murray...that is, Mina...this was written by a sailor.

MINA
My father was a sailor. So was my brother. My mother a sailor's wife. As are my sisters.

ARTHUR
With respect, I am not quite convinced--
QUINCEY
[Needs to hear nothing more.]
Here you go, Miss Murray. I don't think we'll need the whole thing, just the last few weeks. The harbormaster told us this ship, the *Demeter*, was scheduled to arrive from Varna. That's in the Black Sea.

MINA
I know. I shall peruse this and report back to you both with what I learn. If I have time I shall type out a full translation.

ARTHUR
That would indeed be most extremely useful. Many thanks.

SEWARD
I must return to my other patients. Arthur, Quincey—good to see you both. Miss Murray
—please do not hesitate to call upon me at need. My heartfelt hopes news of Mr. Harker arrives very soon. Good day to you all.

> *[Seward exits. FX: A door opens and shuts. All sounds of this parlor, including the clock, totally cease.]*

Scene 5

> *[Mina's room in Hillingham House. Enter Mina. FX: Sound of a very old school manual typewriter.]*

MINA
Transcript of final entries from the Captain's log of the schooner *Demeter*.
12 July. Through the Dardanelles on way to Whitby from Varna. Carrying fifty boxes of clay to Whitby, England. Crew dissatisfied about something. Mate cannot make out what is wrong. Crew are mostly Russian. First Mate Romanian. I have served with each of these men before now. Why are they afraid?

> *[FX: Shipboard sounds below typewriter, swelling at times. Creak of wood. Waves and wind.]*

15 July. Petrofsky missing. Relieved from watch last night but never made it to bunk. Third

Mate says there is a stranger aboard ship, says he saw such a man. Had crew search ship stem to stern. No one found. Men seem more relaxed now. I feel more worried.

22 July. Rough weather for five days. All hands busy with sails. What calm they gained after searching the ship begins to fade. Passing Gibraltar tomorrow. Another man also now missing.

24 July. Well into Bay of Biscay. Another man lost, this time during another tempest. Men too busy to be afraid. We are making excellent time, at least.

30 July. Two days of fog. No other ships to be seen. Crew tired. Both man of watch and steersman gone in middle of night. Mate and I agreed to go armed. Some darkness hovers over this ship. Rare to lose even one crewman. We are only four now from a beginning of nine. The men fear they know not what. As do I.

> *[FX: Sounds of a storm. Then, a man's scream.]*

1 August. Woke up to sounds of a cry. Rushed on deck. Could see nothing in fog. One more crewman vanished, God Help Us! Mate believes us near straits of Dover. I am not sure. No land is visible.

> *[FX: Storm sounds fade. Sounds of a ship continue.]*

3 August. Some doom lies over this ship. Yet another man now gone. We are adrift during the day. Winds rise every night. This is not natural. Even the air feels wrong.

4 August. Mate agitated after coming from below near sunset. Screamed he had learned the secret and only the sea could save him. Then threw himself overboard.

> *[FX: Splashing sounds as something hits the water. Sounds of the ship fade. The typewriter stops.]*

Am alone now.

Scene 6

> *[Day. Garden at Hillingham House Enter Lucy and Arthur. FX: Day birds, footsteps on gravel.]*

ARTHUR
Lucy? Mina said you were out here in the garden. You're looking much better.

LUCY
We never used to lie to one another. Wishing death away won't work, dearest.

ARTHUR
But what can we do but try?

LUCY

Let me be your wife, Arthur. Wrap it up in all the ceremonies you like, or simply pick me up and take me to bed this very minute. I've ceased caring. Moments are all we have, and anything but an unlimited number of those. Why do you hesitate?

ARTHUR

We have time.

LUCY

The Angel of Death is near. Like a promise of sleep and everlasting dreams. Until then, we have today. This minute. This hour. Take it.

ARTHUR

We have duty.

LUCY

No one is asking you to betray the Queen. Only embrace the woman you love. Take me in your
arms, Arthur. Come with me, and be with me.

ARTHUR

I shall. Will all my heart and soul. When we are married. My father has agreed.

LUCY

Arthur! *[She begins to cough.]*

[FX: The sounds of the garden fade.]

<u>**Scene 7**</u>

[Interior Hillingham House, continuous. Mina and Quincey discovered. FX: The parlor clock ticks in the background.]

MINA

You should probably not be spying on Lucy and Arthur, Mr. Morris.

QUINCEY

Old habit. Been his bodyguard since we were seventeen. His father's idea.

MINA

I thought the two of you friends.

QUINCEY

We are, almost brothers by now. But none of Arthur's real brothers were available, and Lord Godalming didn't much care for watching after his son himself. So, hire a companion. Who could fight. What about you and Miss Lucy?

MINA

Does that mean you see Arthur as a bodyguard does? Or yourself as a fellow aristocrat?

QUINCEY

Both. In more ways that you might expect. And to be honest, between the two of us Arthur is the better with a gun. Which is saying something. Any news about your fiancee?

MINA

Jonathan is en route home, exhausted but well. His client must have paid him extremely well, I gather. He wrote quite a long telegram.

QUINCEY

Good news, then! *[A beat.]* What?

MINA

He warned me to go nowhere near Carfax, the property for which he brought the final papers for sale abroad. No details, at least nothing explicit. My impression is that the man who purchased Carfax is dangerous. I have done my own research at the library. In truth I had already begun to do so soon after Jonathan left.

> *[FX: A chair moving, followed by the opening of a desk drawer. Mina hands a book to Quincey.]*

QUINCEY

[Reading]
"An Account of the Legends of in Moldavia, Wallachia and Transylvania."

MINA

Transylvania is where he went on his business errand. It is near Hungary. The name 'Dracula' is mentioned again and again. Such is the name of the person Jonathan was to meet. Evidently a notorious family in that part of the world. A dynasty of ferocious warlords, some said to sold their soul. The name even means "Son of the Devil."

QUINCEY

Is Harker a superstitious man? Or of nervous disposition?

MINA

The precise opposite.

QUINCEY

This Dracula, he's probably just some evil old man, and your Jonathan saw that. Is warning people away. Not like the world has a short supply of evil old men. Hell, Arthur and me work for some.

> *[FX: Door opens and closes. Enter Arthur]*

ARTHUR

Quince, I think we should go send another telegram to the Consulate in Buda-Pesth.

MINA

I should tell you—I've had news of Jonathan.

ARTHUR

Indeed? Good news, I hope?

MINA

He has been ill, but is now retracing his steps back to Whitby as rapidly as he can manage.

ARTHUR

How...wonderful. Yet I think some clarification from the Consulate might be of some use. Quince?

QUINCEY

Miss Murray, no doubt we'll talk later. And I look forward to meeting the man you chose as a husband.

ARTHUR

Sun will be setting in an hour or so. Want to get that telegram off today. Mina, good day. Thank you again for the transcript of the Captain's log. Most illuminating. Again, good day.

[FX: Opening a door, then closing it.]

Scene 8

[Inside a hansom cab. Enter Quincey and Arthur. FX: The muffled click-clop of a horse, the slight sway of the carriage itself.]

QUINCEY

So what was all that about? *[Pause. Arthur does not answer.]* Okay, just have figure it out for myself. Not too hard, as it happens.

ARTHUR

Wish you wouldn't, Quince.

QUINCEY

Lucy thinks she's not long for this world. Hell, odds are at least even. And she wants to be with a man while she's still breathing. Can't say I blame her. I can blame you, though. For being a great big fool.

ARTHUR

Guilty. As per usual.

QUINCEY

Miss Mina's fiancee. Bet you the two of them are going to get married almost

the hour he gets home. No formal announcements in the newspaper, no
waiting a decent period, no elaborate plans.

ARTHUR
Miss Murray and Mister Harker are not burdened with the social status I and
Lucy enjoy.

QUINCEY
They're in love. And free. So are you and Lucy.

ARTHUR
We are not free.

QUINCEY
Say, you ever met this Jonathan Harker?

ARTHUR
No.

QUINCEY
Well, Miss Mina sure is head over heels. And Miss Lucy trusted him to take
care of an important piece of business for her. I am impressed with the both of
them. Met ambassadors and millionaires with less sense. We both have.

ARTHUR
Your point?

QUINCEY
Harker's telegram told Miss Mina never to go anywhere near Carfax. Ever.
Hinted at something really wrong with this Count Dracula, the man who bought
the place. What?

ARTHUR
The harbormaster said the cargo from the _Demeter_ has been picked up. Its
destination was
Carfax.

QUINCEY
And what was that cargo again?

ARTHUR
Fifty boxes of clay, or soil.

QUINCEY
Dirt. Somebody paid to ship fifty boxes of dirt from one side of Europe to the
other?

ARTHUR
I have my doubts. Evidently someone did stow away on the _Demeter_ to kill the
crew...but why? Makes less sense than shipping fifty boxes of dirt! If those
boxes did in fact contain nothing but dirt.

QUINCEY
Which neither one of us believes.

ARTHUR

Quite right. But how would anyone successfully hide on a ship the size of a schooner for three
or four weeks? No, it must have been the First Mate.

QUINCEY

Who killed himself.

ARTHUR

But then, who killed the Captain and steered the ship into Whitby harbor?
Another accomplice, must have been. Whom the Captain believed vanished,
because the Mate told him so. And then fled the ship once it made landfall.
Which seems...absurd.

QUINCEY

Unless the whole thing is a coincidence?

ARTHUR

The log must be a fabrication. Must be.

QUINCEY

Funny. How you can be so smart, and such a fool at the same time?

ARTHUR

Quince, will you please--

QUINCEY

If Lucy looked at me, the way she looks at you, I would not hesitate.

[FX: Sounds of the carriage fade.]

Scene 9

*[Dr. Seward's office. Enter Seward.
FX: The ticking of the clock there, as
the machinery of the phonograph
begins.]*

SEWARD

Ellen Renfield. Charity case, a seamstress who collapsed screaming almost
four weeks ago in Halifax. Long been considered 'odd' there. Endures visions.
Maybe waking nightmares. Religious mania perhaps. Maybe some hysteria in
the blood. She suffers. Her symptoms have grown acute over the last five
days. She obsesses over blood. Will only eat meat if it is burnt dry. Also fears
nighttime, in part due to severe nightmares. Laudanum helps her sleep, as
indeed it does me. The difference, I need no one's permission. So I am
reduced. By one word. "No." I allow Renfield her few drops. Have given
myself the limit of taking myself only as many as I give her. Let us see if that
is wise. I am pleased she is here. I will do all I can to relieve her distress.

*[FX: Sounds of the phonograph and
office abruptly fade.]*

Scene 10

*[The sky above Whitby. Enter Dracula,
Lucy and Mina. FX: The Vampire
Sound. Huge leathern wings that stop
as Dracula lands on a balcony, Voices
speak through glass, from a room on
the other side of the window.]*

MINA

[Muffled slightly by glass]
Never quite sure if your mother approved of me.

LUCY

[Muffled slightly by glass]
Poor Mamma. I look back at her now, and think how unhappy she must have
been. She vented those feelings towards us all, especially after she watched
Papa die.

MINA

That imperious manner she had—it proved useful when dealing with unruly
girls.

LUCY

I always admired you for that. Still do. *[A beat.]* Mina, I have some news for
you.

MINA

[Senses what is coming]
It can wait.

LUCY

I spoke with Mr. Hawkins.

MINA

As did I. Turns out I know more at this point about Jonathan than he does, and
even more about this man who purchased Carfax!

LUCY

I changed my will.

MINA

Hush, now. I shall take these cups of hot chocolate now and leave you to your
sleep. You shall wake refreshed, and stronger. Good night dear Lucy. And
don't be so afraid.

LUCY

Afraid?

MINA

I pray for you. But you know that. Good night.

[FX: A door opens and closes.]

DRACULA

I am here.

[FX: The door to the balcony opens.]

LUCY

There you are. I wondered if I would see you again. Or when. Am I to die tonight?

DRACULA

I do not believe you will.

LUCY

You do not know?

DRACULA

Not yet. Many things are hidden from my kind.

LUCY

The limits you describe are so strange.

DRACULA

Perhaps. Once, long ago. I sought to understand them.

LUCY

Did you ever?

DRACULA

If ever I did, then I have forgotten. When the sun emerges I must sleep, and when it sets I rise. I may not enter a home unless invited by one who dwells there, or owns it. Unless of course the home is mine. I cannot rest without the earth of the place which was home to me in life.

LUCY

That is what I find most surprising.

DRACULA

What? The earth? I think it might be alchemical.

LUCY

That you were once a man.

DRACULA

My fathers and grandfathers were Princes, remote offspring of the great and terrible Attila. I saw battles, even if their names have faded. Commanded armies, although my deeds are now a mere tales to be told, and I can neither confirm nor deny the truth of them.

LUCY

Were you happy, O Azrael? When you were a man?

DRACULA

I do not remember. Are you?

LUCY

Almost. I have one thing I yet long for. After, then I shall bid you enter.

DRACULA

Are you why I am here? Let me but kiss you, and I shall give you wings.

LUCY

Azrael, you are Temptation! Maybe not Azreal after all, but Beelzebub?

DRACULA

Neither are my name. Your company is pleasing. I offer you the chance to be Death even as I am. To wander in dreams and command the wind, to fly from age to age, and watch the shadows
of this world flicker by.

LUCY

I am not ready to go.

DRACULA

Let me kiss you, and you will remain yet. For a time. Each night I would kiss you. There would be no pain. And you would change, a bit at a time, then walk within the nights, learning of her secrets. I do not make this offer often. Many are those who have gone mad so far from the sun, lost in the waking dream. I do not believe this would be your fate.

LUCY

No pain? And time enough to get what I want.

DRACULA

But no guarantees you will succeed.

LUCY

I understand, Azrael. In truth I would rather die in the way you offer than as my parents did. My greatest hope left in life begins to fade. All that I own is better in another's hands. Come into my home. I bid you welcome.

> *[FX: We hear Dracula step into the room...the sounds of the night fade.]*

Scene 11

> *[Aboard a train. FX: A railroad engine begins to move, with the blow of a train whistle, heard from within the train itself. The clacking of the car on the tracks. Someone rustles a newspaper.]*

JONATHAN
[Reading aloud, increasingly focused and worried]
"In a sequel to the strange events of last week, the late Captain of the schooner *Demeter*, that ran aground within Whitby harbor, has now had his funeral. Various local captains carried the casket of this gallant, if foreign, mariner to his final rest. The general atmosphere has been one of grave respect for the fallen man, with many persons of all walks of life attending the procession.

According to our correspondent, the sole cargo aboard the wreck was fifty boxes of what was described as mould, and was consigned to a local solicitor on behalf of the owner. No word as to the owner's identity, save a rumor he has purchased some local property."

[FX: Putting the papers aside, then a fob watch is taken out and opened, the slight steady ticking can be heard.]

Six days old! He is there. In Carfax with the boxes. Might as well be inside another castle. Five hours to York, at best speed. Five and a half more like. Then two hours to Whitby. So. Seven hours, maybe eight. The sun will be setting. Should I have sent a telegram? No. Nothing I can do. But wait. And plan. And hope. And pray. This damn book—the best on the subject and yet hardly a solid fact anywhere. I barely know more now than in the convent. Rest. And pray. Seven hours. Maybe eight. Rest. Get ready. Need to be ready.

[FX: The sounds of the train fade into silence.]

Scene 12

[Parlor at Hillingham House. Midday. FX: The ticking of a clock.]

ARTHUR
You should never have let her attend that funeral! It was clearly too much for her!

MINA
I invite you to attempt to make Lucy refrain from what she has decided upon.

ARTHUR
Why else are you here, then?

QUINCEY
Art! Stop it!

ARTHUR
You...are correct.

QUINCEY
You owe Miss Mina your apology.

ARTHUR
Of course. Miss Murray, my apologies. If my words...no, my words did indeed hurt and insult. Such was their intention. No excuses. Merely abject apologies. Sincere, albeit meager.

MINA
Apology accepted.

ARTHUR

Thank you.

[FX: A door opens. Enter Seward.]

Jack! What news?

SEWARD

Lucy has taken a serious turn for the worse. I don't understand quite how, but there it is. She has lost a great deal of blood. There is something I think might work, if you are willing.

ARTHUR

Anything!

SEWARD

This is not without danger.

ARTHUR

No matter!

SEWARD

Not to you. There's a procedure called blood transfusion. I've seen it done. Technically not difficult. It involves deliberately taking blood from one person then injecting it into another. Sometimes, it does work.

MINA

Sometimes?

SEWARD

Yes. The brutal fact is, it can be fatal. Not always, not even most of the time, but it does happen. And no one knows why.

ARTHUR

Shall we begin?

SEWARD

Come with me, then. You'll need to take off your jacket. And roll up your sleeve. This will not be without pain.

[FX: Door opens then shuts. The sounds of the clock fade.]

Scene 13

[Renfield's rooms at the Sanitorium. FX: The sound of some one vomiting into a bucket. That someone is Renfield.]

RENFIELD

God! My Redeemer! Why have you forsaken me?

[FX: Footsteps approach quickly.]

KATE REED
[From outside the door.]
I am coming in!

[A key turns to unlock the door, which swings open and steps enter—those of Kate Reed.]

KATE REED
Miss Renfield! Are you sick? Was this something you ate?

RENFIELD
I can't get rid of it.

KATE REED
Your forehead is normal. And—you barely ate your food.

RENFIELD
Blood! Everything tastes of blood! I can't get it out of my mouth!

KATE REED
Look at me! Come on, then. Open your mouth. Yes, yes—I don't see any blood. If you bit your tongue the bleeding has stopped now.

RENFIELD
I'm not bleeding. I woke and I kept spitting over and over and over again! I hoped the food would cover the taste. But nothing! Everything is blood. Even the air!

KATE REED
But there is no blood here. You can see for yourself.

RENFIELD
I know! I can see! But I still taste it! Unclean! I am unclean! Disgusting!

KATE REED
I shall summon Dr. Seward.

RENFIELD
He isn't here.

KATE REED
Of course he is.

RENFEILD
No. He's at Hillingham House.

KATE REED
How do you know that?

RENFIELD
I don't know. I never know. Lucy Westenra.

KATE REED

What about her?

RENFIELD

She's sick. I think she's dying. Dr. Seward is trying to save her. You and she—
you were friends once.

KATE REED

Yes. But not close.

RENFIELD

Yes. At school. Best friends. Closer than either of you ever had before. For a
time. Then she got close to someone else. Nina something. Broke your heart.

KATE REED

How did you know that?

RENFIELD

Oh god—water!

KATE REED

Here!

> *[FX: Swallowing sounds, almost to the
> point of gagging.]*

RENFIELD

I still taste it! Unclean! Unclean! The Almighty has turned his face from me.
Thou shalt not eat the blood. It is forbidden!

KATE REED

Here. Hold my hand. Pray with me. Father, Who Art In Heaven, Holy Be Thy
Name. Say it with me.

RENFIELD

Father, who art in Heaven.

KATE REED

Holy be thy name.

RENFIELD

Holy be thy name.

KATE REED

When thy kingdom doth come,

RENFIELD

Thy will shall be done, on this Earth

RENFIELD AND KATE REED

As it is in Heaven. Forgive us all our trespasses as we shall strive to forgive
those who trespass against us. Ward us from all temptation, deliver us from all
evil, for thine is the Glory, and the Kingdom, and thine the Power, for ever.
Amen.

KATE REED

[After a time]
Miss Renfield?

RENFIELD

My mouth still tastes of blood.

[FX: Music cue. Transition.]

Scene 14

*[Lucy's bedroom in Hillingham House.
FX: Wind and day birds from an open
window. Breathing of Lucy, which
sounds haggard. Breathing from
Arthur, as if from pain. The sound of
medical instruments being put away.]*

ARTHUR

Jack, was that enough? Do you need to take more?

SEWARD

I believe this sufficient. Providing it does not prove fatal.

QUINCEY

What are the odds?

SEWARD

No one knows for certain. But death occurs approximately one quarter to one
third of all attempts at blood transfusion. Hence my extreme reluctance.

ARTHUR

You didn't seem to take that much.

SEWARD

I fear to give her more lest she go into shock. Yet if she does not reject this,
you will have
preserved her life.

ARTHUR

I would happily give her all the blood I have.

SEWARD

Were it not for the consumption I'd don't believe she'd've been in so much
danger. Except... where did the blood go? Her bed should be covered with it.
Or she should have been coughing it up by the cup-full. Or shown signs of
internal bleeding. Anemia simply does not happen this swiftly, so it cannot be
that.

QUINCEY

What about her neck?

ARTHUR

What? What's that?

SEWARD

There are two small wounds on Lucy's throat. But they cannot be the source of blood loss, even though they do appear quite fresh. She'd be coated in the stuff. Unless—no, that is absurd.

ARTHUR

I'll be the judge of that.

SEWARD

No. You will not.

QUINCEY

Jack, you say its absurd, I believe you. But what was it?

SEWARD

In theory--someone might have applied a series of leeches to those two spots, removing and replacing each as the creatures consumed their fill. Would have taken hours and required at least dozens of the things to achieve, and Lucy would have had to lie there acquiescent the entire time. Grotesque rubbish!

*[FX: Knock on the door, and after a
moment the door opens. Enter Mina.]*

MINA

Doctor Seward, a message just arrived from your sanitorium. A patient needs your attention. Her name is Renfield and she is reported as having hallucinations.

SEWARD

Thank you.

MINA

How is Lucy?

SEWARD

The blood transfusion is likely to have made a significant difference. However, we shall not know for hours if her body is accepting it. If she lives through the night, we may safely presume she has left any immediate danger behind. Now, I must leave.

ARTHUR

Leave?

SEWARD

There is at present nothing more I can do. Lucy shall either rally, or not. Meanwhile I have another patient, and another duty. As you both should know too well, duty is not a thing I shirk for personal convenience or preference.

QUINCEY

We know that. Don't we, Art?

ARTHUR

Yes. And Jack—thank you for allowing me to do this much for Lucy.

SEWARD

Thank me if it works. If she rouses, I do think she'd like to see your face.

MINA

I'll show you out. Dr. Seward.

[FX. Door closes. Exit Mina and Seward.]

QUINCEY

Jack, he is spooked something fierce.

ARTHUR

I suppose so.

QUINCEY

You just listen for a moment. Jack asked Lucy to marry him. You know that, right? I mean, if I know it, you must.

ARTHUR

Yes.

QUINCEY

He's not a man to do that lightly.

ARTHUR

Neither am I.

QUINCEY

Me neither. Three of us have a lot in common. We all found that out in Egypt. So turn it around. If Miss Lucy had said yes to Jack and no to you, how'd you feel?

ARTHUR

You've made your point, Quince.

[FX: Sounds of winds and the day from the window fade.]

Scene 15

[Renfield's rooms in the sanitorium. FX: Key turns in a lock, then a door opens.]

SEWARD

Miss Renfield? Are you awake?

RENFIELD

I have been trying to sleep. Without success.

SEWARD

May I come in?

RENFIELD

Yes.

[FX: Footsteps enter room.]

SEWARD

May I bring in some light?

RENFIELD

The light, it hurts.

SEWARD

I need to see your appearance. Only a little bit, I promise.

RENFIELD

Yes.

[FX: A match is struck.]

SEWARD

You sound quite exhausted. Would you prefer me to give you something to help you sleep?

RENFIELD

I don't know. I can barely move, yet I fear my dreams.

SEWARD

Tell me about your dreams. And please excuse me while I take your pulse.

RENFIELD

Everything looks unreal. I can see in the dark. I can fly. But I am not human.

SEWARD

An owl perhaps?

RENFIELD

No. But I am a hunter. A demon. Or...something. I find people and kill them. An old man in the graveyard, old and sick and drunk. A sad woman with red hair and black eyes. Wearing violet. She was coughing a good deal. I held her in my arms and killed her with a kiss.

SEWARD

When was this?

RENFIELD

A few nights ago. My mouth tastes of blood.

SEWARD

Miss Reed will bring you some laudanum, and some freshly baked bread. You need to keep up your strength. You are a seamstress as I recall?

RENFIELD

I was.

SEWARD

You still are. Unemployed at the moment, but I shall make efforts to find you a position when you leave here.

RENFIELD

If I do.

SEWARD

You shall. Believe that, and it will help you. May I sit?

RENFIELD

Yes.

[FX: Movement of a chair.]

SEWARD

Seven years ago I was not a doctor, but an Army lieutenant. I had a very good education as it turns out, the dutiful gift of my father. Saw my first real military action. Never mind about the stories of gallantry and heroism in the face of danger. I suppose there must have been plenty of both, but I did not see it. Rather, I and a handful of others ended up trapped behind enemy lines, hiding in an old hotel, defending it against any lone soldiers wandering by. Then, of necessity, hiding the bodies. Little food. Little water. Just fear and boredom and gnawing hunger. Within a few days, I found a great deal of clarity by imagining my future, by picturing it in my mind, and determining each hour was but a few more steps in my journey to that future. It worked. I survived, and felt no surprise. Eventually the fighting ended. I resigned my commission, and determined to work in medicine, to help my fellow men rather than wound, or kill them.

RENFIELD

Your father.

SEWARD

Yes, he paid for more schooling.

RENFIELD

And never congratulated you.

SEWARD

No.

RENFIELD

He never saw anything he would find distressing. The colors or flowers or food he disliked were nowhere near his person. The same with the illegitimate offspring of a youthful mistresses he grew tired of. Gave money, not affection, never love.

SEWARD

Who has told you these things?

RENFIELD

I know so much I would rather not. Your grief at falling in love, then having her reject you. Your anger at losing even one patient. That is as a fire. It burns.

SEWARD

All very well and good, but who in the staff has been talking to you? About events? And about me?

RENFIELD

Only you, Doctor Seward. Only you. And you do not believe me. I'm sorry.

SEWARD

I must ask again--

RENFIELD

Death, he rides not a pale horse but flies on leather wings. Soon you will believe. So sorry. I wish you did not have to. Guns cannot touch him. A sword, though, that may save us all from him.

SEWARD

From who precisely?

RENFIELD

He who died and arose, and in the name of Hell became Death.

> *[FX: After a moment or two, footsteps move and the door opens then closes. Footsteps fade in the hallway.]*

Scene 16

> *[Office of Dr. Seward. FX: Ticking of a clock. Distant sounds of a harbor—waves, seagulls, a bell. Knock on a door.]*

SEWARD

Enter.

> *[Enter Kate Reed. FX: Door opens, closes.]*

KATE REED

You sent for me sir?

SEWARD

Yes, Miss Reed. Take a seat.

KATE REED

Thank you, sir.

> *[FX: Chair is moved.]*

SEWARD

You seem interested in my collection.

KATE REED

I did not mean to stare.

SEWARD

No need to apologize. Truth is, I sometimes forget they are even here. Do you know what this is?

KATE REED

Some kind of bird with a man's head. A monster? A demon?

SEWARD

It is called a "Ba." The ancient Egyptians thought this is what a human soul looked like, traveling between the body and heaven.

KATE REED

That does not sound right.

SEWARD

The Egyptians were not Christian, Miss Reed. They had their own ways of looking at life and death, ways not like ours. I assume you recognize this?

KATE REED

A snake stone.

SEWARD

Exactly so. Remnants of animals from a different age of the earth, once plentiful but now vanished.

KATE REED

I don't know about that.

SEWARD

This one here is my most treasured item. Can you guess what it is? My father left this to me in his will. His collection was much larger, most of it now in the British Museum.

KATE REED

It is a bottle.

SEWARD

Of a kind. This vial is supposed to contain the tears of Saint Veronica.

KATE REED

Sorry to hear you've lost your father.

SEWARD

Thank you. I've been asking about your work here, Miss Reed. What I'm told seems quite positive. You've mostly worked with our charity cases, I believe?

KATE REED

Yes, sir.

SEWARD

And you take the time to talk with them, to chat as it were, to give the gift of normalcy to those who suffer from its lack. Admirable. I would go so far as to say 'commendable.'

KATE REED

Thank you very much.

SEWARD

In this context, gossip has its place. However, I must draw the line at gossip about me.

KATE REED

Sir

SEWARD

Earlier today Renfield repeated details about my life, details I had not in fact shared with anyone at all. How that information became the stuff of local gossip, while disturbing, is not nearly so appalling as that a member of my staff shared it with a patient. There must be trust in the practice of medicine, Miss Reed. Trust offered, and trust earned. What have you to say for yourself?

KATE REED

I do apologize, sir! It seemed harmless enough. I thought it nothing.

SEWARD

Nothing?

KATE REED

I am most miserably sorry, Dr. Seward. The fact I know, or knew, one of your private patients
seemed as obscure and harmless a bit of news as possible to share. Or very nearly.

SEWARD

You speak of Miss Westenra?

KATE REED

Yes, sir.

SEWARD

You know her? She shares things with you?

KATE REED

Oh, no. We haven't spoken in years. And we were...that it, we were not close. The Westenras, sir, are a people commonly spoken of here. Famous even. And I revealed none of her secrets, not least because I don't know any. Just what everyone knows.

SEWARD

Everyone?

KATE REED

Yes.

SEWARD

[Taking a moment]
Is it then common knowledge I proposed marriage to the lady?

KATE REED

You? What? No. No! I never knew that! Not till this moment! Unless this is some kind of test, sir? I don't know what to say.

SEWARD

Unfortunately, Miss Reed, I believe you. I say unfortunately because now I am left with an even more disturbing query. Namely, how did Renfield know this? She's received no visitors I believe?

KATE REED

Not one, sir.

SEWARD

And yet she knew Mrs. Singleton died the other night. Described her in sufficient detail to leave no doubt. And somehow also knew about that old tramp found dead near the Abbey. That was in the newspapers, of course. What? Miss Reed? Speak up!

KATE REED

Dr. Seward, sir. The other day Renfield said something about me, about something that happened in the past. No one knew about this. Well, except me and one other. I simply cannot make out how she knew about it. It should be impossible.

SEWARD

What was it she said?

KATE REED

Please do not ask me that, sir. It is of an extremely personal nature.

SEWARD

[After a pause]
You may go, Miss Reed.

> *[FX: Chair moves. Steps. A door opens, then closes.]*

Scene 17

> *[Parlor, Hillingham House. Quincey and Mina. FX: Ticking of the parlor clock.]*

MINA

My family moved from York back to Whitby when I was twelve. There was a fire and we'd lost our livelihood as well as a sister. The following year I started attending school with Lucy and we became close. Children, perhaps you have noticed, do not forgive other children for being too clever.

QUINCEY
My guess is you're not fond of your own students.

MINA
Not greatly. But I do enjoy my position.

QUINCEY
And how did you meet Mr. Jonathan Harker?

MINA
At a library. Is there a purpose to this line of inquiry, Mr. Morris?

QUINCEY
Curiosity. Must say I feel impressed with both you and Miss Lucy. But then the ladies I end up
 spending most of my time around aren't nearly as interesting. They don't reveal any such thing, anyway.

MINA
Where do you meet them?

QUINCEY
A mix. High society events where everybody is pretending to be better than they are. Or grimy, dangerous places where they're all pretending to be worse. Art and me, we have to travel a lot.

MINA
Which are you? Pretending to be better than you are, or pretending to be worse?

[FX: Door opens. Enter Jonathan.]

MINA
Dear God. Thank you.

JONATHAN
I returned as fast as was possible.

MINA
Walk though I may within the valley of the shadow of death...

JONATHAN
We shall fear no evil.

[FX: Harker drops his single piece of luggage. The sound of a single kiss.]

I'm interrupting something.

QUINCEY

Not really.

MINA

Jonathan, this is Mr. Quincey Morris, a friend of Arthur Holmwood, Lucy's fiancee.

QUINCEY

Honored to meet you, Mr. Harker. And welcome home!

MINA

We are waiting for news about Lucy. Arthur, that is, Mr. Holmwood, is with her now. She's been
very weak of late.

JONATHAN

Weak? Has anything changed? Have you been receiving new visitors? Or going anywhere different?

MINA

No. She's been in Arthur's company of course, which often means she's been with Quincey. She began using a new doctor about a week after you left, the man who runs the lady's sanitorium, Dr. Jack Seward.

QUINCEY

Who turns out to be an old friend of myself and Art. We were in Egypt together during the war.

JONATHAN

Has she been near Carfax?

MINA

Not at all. Neither have I, nor anyone else as far as I know.

JONATHAN

Good. But the _Demeter_. I read it ran aground. With boxes of soil? Everyone on board missing or dead?

QUINCEY

That's right. You know about that?

[FX: A door opens and enter Arthur.]

ARTHUR

Excuse me?

QUINCEY

Art, this here is Miss Mina's long lost fiancee. Finally back.

ARTHUR

[Shifting modes]
Oh I see! Well, that does explain the hands clasped together as if neither one will ever let go. Welcome home Mr. Harker.

MINA

How is Lucy?

JONATHAN

Yes, how is she?

ARTHUR

Many times improved, I am happy to say! She and I were just chatting a bit. She looks and sounds utterly splendid.

QUINCEY

Good to know the transfusion worked.

ARTHUR

I as well!

JONATHAN

Excuse me. Transfusion? I don't know this word.

QUINCEY

Dr. Jack Seward did it. Said it was dangerous, but...well. It worked. He transferred blood from Art here into Lucy. Her consumption, she had a real bad spell.

JONATHAN

I did not know that was possible, to do that.

ARTHUR

Neither did I. Fortunately for us all it was, and is! I'll admit to filling pretty damn weak and sick myself, at least for now.

JONATHAN

I was wondering at your face. At how pale you look. Wondered why.

ARTHUR

Well, if you will forgive me... I was myself wondering. At your attire, Mr. Harker.

JONATHAN

All my luggage I had to leave behind at the castle.

ARTHUR

Castle?

JONATHAN

Castle Dracula. That is where I went on behalf of Lucy. I barely escaped once Count Dracula left.

ARTHUR

Escaped? Sounds like you had an adventure!

JONATHAN

I was left alone. Locked in a room. In the end, I had to crawl out a window to the ground below. That took, I don't know how long.

QUINCEY

How far were you from the nearest town?

JONATHAN

Miles and miles. Eventually I found a convent. When I said the name "Dracula" they almost turned me away. Should have known better by then. The things I saw there. I don't have the words. Count Dracula is a very evil person, capable I think of perhaps any sin you can imagine, and much more besides. Charming, to be sure. Extremely intelligent. Almost a poet, really. But, evil. Please believe me.

MINA

Always.

ARTHUR

Of course, but he is not here, after all.

JONATHAN

I think he is.

MINA

He bought Carfax. That was the whole reason Jonathan journeyed there. Lucy was looking to sell the estate and an agent for this foreign nobleman was willing to pay the price she asked.

JONATHAN

And he could easily afford it. He bade me fill my pockets before he left. And I did.

*[FX: Sound of numerous coins
dropping onto a table.]*

ARTHUR

Is that--?

JONATHAN

Gold. There were piles of it everywhere. In Buda-pesth, after leaving the hospital, I bought
local clothes. No doubt I look quite bizarre.

ARTHUR

Tell you what, Harker—allow me to purchase a new suit! You'll look a tad less...well...foreign. Never been to Buda-pesth, myself. Plenty of other places, but not there. Cairo, Istanbul, Venice...

JONATHAN

But—said you gave your blood to Lucy? That sounds extreme. Was her need that dire?

ARTHUR

Unfortunately.

JONATHAN

And she is better?

QUINCEY

Mr. Harker, I've got a question for you. And I'd like an immediate answer it you don't mind. Your throat.

JONATHAN

Yes?

QUINCEY

You've got an old wound there, or a pair of them. Almost healed into scars. Right on the side of your throat. There. You see, Art?

MINA

Let me see. Oh!

ARTHUR

No, no, no, no! No, that is impossible.

MINA

What happened to you?

ARTHUR

They are the same. Exactly the same.

MINA

The same as what?

ARTHUR

Lucy! They are identical! What in the name of God is going on here?

QUINCEY

Mr. Harker? How did you get those two punctures on your throat?

[FX: All sounds fade as music swells.]

END OF ACT ONE

ACT TWO

Scene 1

[Parlor at Hillingham. Continuous.
FX: The distinctive ticking of this
clock.]

ARTHUR
I will have an answer!. Mr. Harker, how came you to have those wounds upon your throat? Wounds I can frankly say are not unknown to me. Speak! At once!

QUINCEY
Art. Give the man time to answer.

JONATHAN
I fear my answer will not satisfy you. It certainly does not me. While at Castle Dracula I fell into a kind of stupor. After my escape, I was in fairly wild country for a time. When precisely these wounds were inflicted I cannot say. You say Lucy has the same wounds?

ARTHUR
Mr. Harker, I am a medical layman. Would you consent to being examined by Lucy's physician, Dr. Jack Seward? I can send my driver to go fetch him. I presume you quite tired, but please understand Lucy's health is in great jeopardy.

JONATHAN
Of course.

QUINCEY
Do you have a place to stay yet, Harker?

MINA
He has a room here. Lucy put it at his disposal when we became engaged.

ARTHUR
Of course. Rest, why don't you?

JONATHAN
Thank you, I will. You are the son of Lord Godalming, is that right?

ARTHUR
One of them.

JONATHAN
Miss Westenra told me stories about you. Called you daring. A man of action. One used to danger.

ARTHUR
One does one's duty to Queen and Country.

MINA

Do you have any luggage?

JONATHAN

Only what you see.

MINA

If you gentlemen will excuse us?

[FX: Footsteps, a door opens and closes.]

ARTHUR

I'll go tell William to go fetch Jack.

QUINCEY

Ask him to come, you mean.

ARTHUR

William will use the right language, Quince.

[FX: The sounds of the parlor fade.]

Scene 2

[Harker's bedroom at Hillingham. Continuous. FX: Sound of a door opening, two sets of footsteps entering.]

HARKER

Close the door.

[FX: The door firmly shuts.]

MINA

There is much I must tell you.

HARKER

I long to hear ever word. But first, I was lying just now.

MINA

I know.

HARKER

Of course. I remember exactly how I got these wounds on my neck. Exactly. I wish to God I did not. But those men don't know me. They wouldn't believe, and that would be a disaster.

MINA

I will. I do.

HARKER
That I do not doubt. Nor ever will.

MINA
I want to hear every word of what happened. But first, I have news. My love, I am with child. *[Silence.]* Jonathan, please say something.

HARKER
I did not think I could love you more. I did not believe it possible. Until this moment. And I will protect you. Together, we will protect our child. I wish that was not needed, but it is.

MINA
We will be the equal of whatever we face. What?

HARKER
Wish I were sure of that. I am not.

MINA
[Genuinely shocked]
What happened in Transylvania?

HARKER
I met a Devil. Something not human yet walks on the earth. It has a man's voice or at least a human one. But not alive. It is Death. Incarnate. It almost killed me. And it is here, in Whitby, this very hour.

> *[FX: Whatever ambient sounds in this room has now fades, replaced by that of waves hitting a rocky shore. No birds. This in turn fades.]*

Scene 3

> *[Renfield's room. Very soon after. FX: Distant footsteps growing closer from the hall. Turning of pages in a book, accompanied by Renfield's breathing.]*

RENFIELD
[Reading aloud]
"Then I saw a horse the color of bone, and upon that horse rode DEATH, and the legions of Hell did follow after. Power was given onto this one, over shadows and pestilence and hunger, and power also over the winds and beasts of the Earth."

> *[Enter Dracula. FX: The Vampire Sound.]*

RENFIELD

[Reading aloud]

"And he broke the sixth seal, so that thunder echoed over the Earth, the day became as night, and behold for the moon had become red as blood."

DRACULA

Are you the reason I am here?

RENFIELD

Fallen Angel!

DRACULA

I can feel your faith. Are you a witch? Or a saint?

RENFIELD

Get thee behind me!

DRACULA

Fear. You exhale it with each breath. I have seen fear countless times, but had almost forgotten what it felt like. Thank you.

RENFIELD

The Lord God, he shall comfort me and guide me. Walk though I may within the valley of the shadow of death, I shall fear nothing evil.

DRACULA

Not true. But more true than mere moments ago. You hold up your cross, expecting me to fear it, but of course I do not. Crosses are merely a shape. Natural, as I am not.

> *[In some confusion at first, they begin to speak with a similar rhythm to one another.]*

RENFIELD

You wander through this world you once commanded. This fact you raged against?

DRACULA

At first. That was long ago.

RENFIELD

Centuries. How many you are not sure. You mind and soul—they are awash with blood. Thou shalt not eat the blood.

DRACULA

Your mind touched mine while I slept at sea. I saw these walls. And your terror, seeping into me drop by drop. Hardly anything to notice then, but now--

RENFIELD

I can feel your power. Your purpose, as you see it. I can feel your wings.

DRACULA

I can feel your pain. That, I had almost forgot. Pain. We bleed into each other.

RENFIELD

For a time.

DRACULA

Only for a time. I shall leave you soon, and then all I do shall be just an echo.

RENFIELD

Keeping me from sleep, and filling me with fear

DRACULA

Just as you shall echo within me.

RENFIELD

Your voice destroyed my life. I can never get it back. You are immortal and will never leave me.

DRACULA

Until...

RENFIELD

Yes.

DRACULA

For this moment then, because we are here, together, I shall give mercy.

RENFIELD

At this moment, I am strong enough to know that is what I need.

DRACULA

I shall see you again, within the shadows. One day. We shall speak beyond, outside of time. Beyond all pain and regrets.

RENFIELD

You can die?

DRACULA

Even God died, Ellen Renfield.

> *[FX: Perhaps Renfield cries out, in pain and/or pleasure. The Vampire Sound fades leaving silence.]*

Scene 4

> *[Lucy's bedroom. Lucy discovered. Later. FX: Waves in the distance, the rustle of trees, an owl, etc.]*

LUCY

Almost done. Almost.

> *[FX: Knock on door.]*

Come in.

[FX; Door opens. Enter Seward.]

SEWARD

Lucy?

LUCY

Hello Jack!

SEWARD

You should not be in front of an open window, not in your condition.

[FX: Closing of french windows firmly.
Sound of the outdoors fade.]

LUCY

What does that matter, now?

SEWARD

It always matters. Always!

LUCY

Ever the soldier.

SEWARD

I resigned my commission years ago. Who helped you into this chair?

LUCY

Still a soldier, though. You fight death himself. Can I tell you a secret?

SEWARD

I would be honored.

LUCY

I think you much more a hero now than before. What a terrible pity a woman is
not allowed more than one husband. My dashing Jack.

SEWARD

Please do not say that. We need to get you back to bed.

LUCY

You came in here for a reason. Not to get me out from a perfectly comfortable
chair.

SEWARD

Yes. I did want to see you of course.

LUCY

I feel the same.

SEWARD

Jonathan Harker has returned.

LUCY

Mina told me. Most people don't recognize when she's supremely happy, but I do.

SEWARD

May I please examine your neck?

LUCY

Whatever for?

SEWARD

You have a pair of cuts.

LUCY

Insect bites I think. Or maybe I pinned myself in an act of extreme distraction.

SEWARD

Perhaps so. Yes. There they are. Exactly the same size. I now must go. I have some things I must do but my plan is to return.

LUCY

Good.

> *[He exits. FX: The opening of a door, than it shuts.]*

Scene 5

> *[The Hillingham House parlor. FX: That room's clock chimes nine o'clock. Arthur, Mina, Quincey, Jonathan all present.]*

ARTHUR
[Had been waiting for the clock to finish]
As I was saying, Harker, nice to see you in some proper English attire. Doesn't quite fit but I am sure that will change.

MINA

He left his suits here before heading to Transylvania.

QUINCEY

What are your plans, now you're back?

JONATHAN

Marriage.

QUINCEY

Good for you.

ARTHUR

What about your firm? Hawkins and Abbott. Surely they'll be glad to have you back.

JONATHAN

Maybe.

QUINCEY

Whatever else happened, at least you can say you were well paid. All those gold coins make a difference.

JONATHAN

Yes.

QUINCEY

Have you told them what happened?

JONATHAN

No.

[Pause, then Quincey laughs.]

JONATHAN

Something funny.

QUINCEY

You know, I'd love to play poker with you someday.

JONATHAN

I don't know the game.

QUINCEY

I'll teach you.

[FX: Door opens and Seward enters.]

ARTHUR

Jack! I trust you found Lucy well?

SEWARD

She's as she was.

ARTHUR

Good man, good man. Now, if you would be so good as to examine the wounds on Harker's throat here? I would value your opinion very much.

SEWARD

Mr. Harker? Welcome back.

JONATHAN

Thank you Dr. Seward. And thank you for your care of our friend.

SEWARD

Yes. Well, my duty. May I see these mysterious wounds?

JONATHAN

At once.

[FX: Cloth moving.]

SEWARD

Mr. Harker, I must insist you tell me precisely how you gained these wounds. Well, at this point they are really scars, but how did you come by them?

JONATHAN

I don't remember. I was kept prisoner by my host. He eventually left his castle, leaving me locked in a room with no food or water. There was a window. Fortunately. The Holy Sisters who found me said these wounds were already healing by then.

SEWARD

Well, Cover yourself. Arthur, Quincey—the scars on Mr. Harker here are of the exact size and width as those on Miss Lucy.

ARTHUR

And how is that possible?

SEWARD

I actually want to know that more than you do!

QUINCEY

Jack? Why? There's something more, isn't there?

SEWARD

It makes no sense. And I mean that absolutely literally, it makes no sense at all, not one shred.

MINA

What makes no sense?

ARTHUR

Out with it, man.

SEWARD

I've seen these wounds before.

ARTHUR

You've already said as much.

SEWARD

No. On someone else as well. Patient of mine. Mrs. Singleton. Nice enough woman, but having trouble dealing the pressures of motherhood. She was sad, even melancholy. Then, she died. Quite suddenly. We thought she'd caught a cough taking a walk one evening, but in just a day or so...the point being, she had absolutely identical wounds on her throat as well. Absolutely identical. Same size. Same distance. Almost precisely the same location. Of course, in her case, completely unhealed.

ARTHUR

That is...

SEWARD

Bizarre! I know.

MINA

Do you have a theory?

SEWARD

One! The three of you were bitten by exactly the same animal. Hundreds of miles apart. Without anyone seeing it happen. Or the animal itself, which given the size of the bites must be quite large. Which is impossible. So I would be grateful for any suggestions as to a different theory.

JONATHAN

[After a silence]
I may have one.

> *[FX: The sounds of the parlor stop after a few moments.]*

Scene 6

> *[Dr. Seward's office. Day. FX: The ticking of his office's clock as he prepares his phonograph diary. From his open window one an hear the faint sounds of the harbor. He waits a moment or two.]*

SEWARD

[His voice as through a funnel.]
I believe this will be my final entry. Last night Miss Reed found Ellen Renfield dead in her room. She looked pale. On her throat I saw the same two wounds. Harker has a theory, a wild one, but I have nothing better, and it involves a foreigner who purchased Carfax. Maybe he's right. I feel weary. Lucy...Miss Westenra...is no better. Another transfusion helped her rally but little else. I dare not try it again. She may last another day. Maybe two. Or three. I don't know.

> *[FX: Knock on the door.]*

SEWARD

[No longer using a funnel]
One moment!

> *[FX: The smooth putting away of the phonograph.]*

SEWARD

Enter!

> *[FX: Door opens and Kate Reed enters.]*

KATE REED
Dr. Seward, sorry to bother you, sir.

SEWARD
Not at all.

KATE REED
Was wondering if Miss Renfield had any family?.

SEWARD
No. So it will be a pauper's grave, as soon as feasible. Fear of contagion.

KATE REED
When? Do you know?

SEWARD
Tomorrow, at five. Shall we pay our respects together, Miss Reed?

KATE REED
She had no one else, it seems.

SEWARD
She had someone, though. No small thing that, at least. You may go, Miss Reed.

KATE REED
Yes, sir.

[FX: The door opens, closes. The sound of Seward's office fade away.]

Scene 7

[Lucy's bedroom, near dusk. FX: Wind through tree branches and day birds can be heard. Lucy and Mina discovered.]

LUCY
So you are Mrs. Jonathan Harker now?

MINA
I am proud to say it.

LUCY
Wish I were strong enough to have been there.

MINA
Jonathan tried to talk the Vicar into coming here. The old man refused. Not even for an extra fee.

LUCY

What a fool! But how kind of Jonathan to try. And now that we have some proper time together, how did he react to the news?

MINA

As I expected. With great joy.

LUCY

Of course.

MINA

He does have an idea he wants to broach with you?

LUCY

That sounds a little too tempting to be true.

MINA

[Laughs]

Not that! But he is worried. He had a terrible encounter when abroad. The man to whom you sold Carfax proved to be a very strange, even dangerous person who expressed an interest in you. Jonathan at first thought it harmless, a new owner asking about the previous one, who would after all be his neighbor. Later, certain aspects of his man's character came to light.

LUCY

You're not telling me something.

> *[FX: A distinctive knock on the door. After a moment, the door opens. Enter Jonathan.]*

JONATHAN

Lucy? I've managed to talk Mr. Holmwood into agreeing to stay with you tonight while you sleep.

LUCY

You succeeded?

JONATHAN

I asked him to function as your bodyguard. That seemed to quiet his sense of propriety.

LUCY

Probably not enough. Bodyguard against what?

JONATHAN

Intruders.

LUCY

What intruders?

MINA

The man to whom you sold Carfax.

JONATHAN
I may be wrong. He pay pose no specific threat to you at all. But I have seen him do things, commit acts I can only call diabolical.

LUCY
Thank you for your efforts, Jonathan.

[Jonathan and Mina both feel her response to this news is unusual.]

MINA
Diabolical seems the perfect word, from what you've said. I cannot think of a better.

LUCY
How dramatic. So will Quincey be joining Arthur tonight?

MINA
No.

LUCY
Pity.

[FX: Knock on the door. After a moment, the door opens. Enter Arthur.]

LUCY
Arthur! My protector?

ARTHUR
A role I take up only too eagerly.

LUCY
Against foreigners and their evil plans?

ARTHUR
Yes. I don't find that at all amusing, to be honest.

LUCY
Mina, Jonathan—you are but newly married. No doubt you wish to be alone. Go. Be alone, together. Dear Arthur, come draw up a chair. Sit beside me. We will talk and I promise to try not to outrage you. Dear Lord, you look exhausted!

ARTHUR
To sit beside you forever is among the dearest wishes of my heart.

LUCY
You haven't recovered yet. From Jack's transfusion procedure.

ARTHUR
I give you my work of honor I have. I shall sit beside you the night through and keep you safe. I promise.

JONATHAN

We'd best leave.

MINA

Good night, Lucy.

LUCY

I hope so.

JONATHAN

Are you sure you are up to this?

ARTHUR

Quite.

> *[FX: Door opens and closes as they exit.]*

LUCY

Arthur, there's a decanter over there. Could you pour us both a small glass?
The stimulation will
do us both some good I think.

ARTHUR

Yes, of course. You merest wish is my slavish command.

LUCY

Would that were true, my love. But never mind that, now. Get us both a drink.
Just a little bit for me. You take as much as you want.

> *[FX: Sounds of Lucy's bedroom quickly fade.]*

Scene 8

> *[Seward's office. Later. FX: The distinctive ticking of his clock. Liquid poured into two glasses. Seward and Quincey discovered.]*

SEWARD

Sorry I don't have any whiskey.

QUINCEY

I have no problem with brandy.

SEWARD

Here.

> *[FX: The two touch each others' glasses in a mock toast. Seward takes a swallow.]*

QUINCEY
You always hated losing a patient. Even before you were a doctor. Now you've lost two.

SEWARD
No offense, but, in Egypt the pair of you seemed to be enjoying yourselves.

QUINCEY
And you weren't.

SEWARD
No. Why are you here, Quince? We are friends, but you don't really do social visits. Especially when alone.

QUINCEY
Mr. Jonathan Harker. Wanted to talk to you about him. What do you think of him?

SEWARD
I frankly envy a great deal what he and Miss Murray have found together.

QUINCEY
Me, too. Yeah. But the thing is—well he says this Count Dracula is some kind of devil-worshiper. Says the man killed a baby, and seems to believe himself some kind of warlock.

SEWARD
Harker's leaving something out of that story.

QUINCEY
Everyone does.

SEWARD
I suppose. Do you want another?

QUINCEY
Still sipping mine, thanks. Harker thinks this Dracula believes in magic. So, what if we tried using magic against him? I mean, if he believes it will work won't that mean it will work?

SEWARD
Interesting. It does presuppose this Dracula fellow knows what has been done. And you came to me because...? Oh! My collection!

QUINCEY
Better to use the real thing, just in case Dracula would know the difference.

SEWARD
Well! Not invalid as far as I can see.

QUINCEY
He was wondering if there was a ward of some kind we could put in Lucy's bedroom. That I remember from Egypt. The black dog?

SEWARD
Anubis. God of mummification and the dead. Don't think so. Although you can have it if you like. I'm sick of the damn thing. Something to make a Satan-worshiper pause. I think—yes. Yes, this should work. Better than anything else I have.

QUINCEY
Looks like a perfume bottle.

SEWARD
See the liquid inside? Those are supposed to be the genuine tears of a saint.

QUINCEY
Which one?

SEWARD
Veronica. She wept as Jesus was led to the cross, and early Christians gathered her tears in this bottle, then sealed it with wax. Come to think on it, they might well have poured perfume out of the thing first. Why not? More to the point, it looks ancient and revered.

QUINCEY
Should do the trick.

SEWARD
For whatever that is worth. Sorry. I find myself all too sodden with melancholy of late.

QUINCEY
I understand, Jack.

SEWARD
Do you have Arthur's carriage?

QUINCEY
Waiting for us outside.

SEWARD
Let me get my coat.

*[FX: The sounds of Seward's office
fade away.]*

Scene 9

*[The garden attached to Hillingham
House, Enter Lucy. FX: Winds and
night birds.]*

LUCY
Are you here, O Azreal? I am here. Ready and very willing.

*[FX: The sound of wings, which
approach then stop.]*

DRACULA
You are stronger than I believed.

LUCY
I have a very fine and determined doctor. He will be dreadfully disappointed, I fear. Especially when he learns what use I put the sleeping draught he gave me. So shall dear Arthur. But I am so very weary of all this pain. I hate having to work so hard even to breathe.

DRACULA
Some have ever hated and feared me. Others have sought me out. Many ignore my presence with all the will they possess. Still others try in all sorts of ways to bargain with me.

LUCY
Does it make a difference?

DRACULA
Ultimately, no.

LUCY
You bargained with me.

DRACULA
I made you an offer. Because you saw me, knew me, yet did not flee or rage or weep. You merely said--

LUCY
Hello. Well, I've been expecting your visit for years.

DRACULA
Maybe you are why I am here. I shall take all the pain of your flesh away.

> *[FX: A heartbeat, which rises in tempo, then slows, then stops. Sound of someone hitting the ground. Sounds of the night fade away.]*

Scene 10

> *[Parlor at Hillingham House, day. Mina, Arthur, Seward, Quincey are all present. FX: The usual clock. Sounds of day—birds, mostly—from the window.]*

MINA
Is there any doubt, Dr. Seward?

SEWARD
None. I gave Lucy that sleeping powder earlier that day. There was residue in

the decanter. I told her blending the powder with any kind of wine or spirit would hasten the effect.

ARTHUR

Yes, but why?

SEWARD

She must have wanted you to sleep. She saw how ragged you looked. How exhausted. Unafraid for herself, she made sure you had that rest she knew your body so needed. Were she not so utterly fearless, she would not have been Lucy.

MINA

When we met she could be timid. I thought for a time she was trying to become invisible. Until we grew to know one another.

ARTHUR

Yes. Between the two of us, she was the less reckless one. At first. Losing her parents changed her.

[FX: The clock chimes one o'clock. Door opens. Enter Jonathan.]

JONATHAN

The carriages are here. Shall we be going?

MINA

Yes. Dr. Seward—Jack--would you be so kind as to allow us to bring you?

DR. SEWARD

Thank you. That is very kind of you, Miss Murray. I am sorry—Mrs. Harker.

QUINCEY

Come along, Art. Finish your drink.

[FX: A quick swallow of some liquid, followed by the door closing. After a few more moments, the sounds of the parlor fade.]

Scene 11

[The graveyard, not far from the sea. That night. FX: Distant waves. Wind whistling amid the mausoleums. Footsteps. Enter Kate Reed.]

KATE REED

No wonder they put a graveyard here. Who else but dead people would put up with this? *[FX: Footsteps stop. A pause.]* Hello Lucy. We never did get to see each other again. Right silly of me to expect it. Two funerals in one week. The other was a patient of mine. Nice, sad lady. I don't think we helped her much. Wish I could have helped you. Remember how we'd talk about stories? About maidens getting rescued from dragons or some such? Walking up here, this idea came to mind. Sometimes you hear about rich folk getting buried with bells, just in case they were buried alive. I had this notion I'd get here, and you'd be ringing that kind of bell. I'd hear you and get help. Be the hero. Your hero. Silly. But—all the same. I'm listening. *[Pause.]* Silly. You used to call me that. I called you worse, later. But if you'd rung a bell, I would've helped. Somehow.

[Enter Lucy. FX: The Vampire Sound.]

LUCY

Katie? Katie Reed?

KATE REED

Oh my god!

LUCY

I opened my eyes and heard a voice. A familiar one but I did not recognize it at first.

KATE REED

What are you...how did you get here? I was just day dreaming about you being buried alive!

LUCY

A dream! Yes, of course. He told me.

KATE REED

Lucy—how did you get out of the tomb? Are you alright? Did you hurt yourself?

LUCY

You said such sweet words. I hurt you, didn't I? Long ago? When we barely more than children?

KATE REED

Yes. But...but that was a long time past.

LUCY

I am sorry. For everything. For my hurting you, even if I was too stupid to realize that's what I did.

KATE REED

How can you be here?

LUCY

I don't really know. But I am. Let me hold you. Weep if you need. Or smile. We shall comfort one another. As once we did. Two orphans or near orphans, sans family or friends.

KATE REED

I don't understand.

LUCY

Remember how we used to hold each other like this? Two lonely girls in that grim, dark school?

KATE REED

Yes.

LUCY

So alone, far from home.

KATE REED

I remember. We were sisters.

LUCY

And we can be again.

[FX: The wind, the distant surf, and the Vampire Sound all fade.]

Scene 12

[Hillingham House parlor. Later that night. Quincey, Arthur, Seward, Mina, Jonathan all enter. FX: The clock.]

QUINCEY

You want some more whiskey?

ARTHUR

Don't think so. Can hardly feel a thing now.

MINA

Perhaps now you can sleep?

ARTHUR

Maybe.

JONATHAN

Mr. Holmwood, you are very welcome to sleep here tonight. Don't bother with a carriage ride back to your hotel.

SEWARD

For what it is worth, I think Harker has the right idea.

ARTHUR

Unconsciousness sounds appealing right this moment.

QUINCEY

Come along then.

[Quincey and Arthur exit. FX: A door opens, then closes.]

MINA
I do hope he sleeps well. With dreams of happiness he does not remember when awake.

JONATHAN
You are kindness, and wisdom.

SEWARD
Harker, I am not totally persuaded. Frankly what you're suggesting sounds grotesque.

JONATHAN
It is grotesque. And, I'm afraid, probably necessary.

SEWARD
Only probably?

MINA
Dr. Seward, please consider that even I think Jonathan's suggestion has a horrible logic to it.

JONATHAN
May I make my case?

JONATHAN
Granted, my memories of Castle Dracula and what happened there remain incomplete. But what I do recall is the stuff of waking nightmares. Criminal perversion at the very least. I would like to think this nothing more than dreams or delirium.

SEWARD
Which it probably is.

JONATHAN
Except for the reaction any time I mentioned the name Dracula. In Bistritz, they looked at me as if I'd just confessed to eating human flesh. The Nuns at the Convent who treated me gasped in horror and insisted on filling my room with garlic wreaths and religious icons. What reasons they gave sound absurd, all about his being an immortal wizard or monster or something, but their fear —that, I swear was genuine, and from what I could see universal. Something inspired that. Nothing good.

SEWARD
With respect, that remains circumstantial.

JONATHAN
When Dracula's personal cargo arrived in Whitby, it was aboard a ship with the entire crew missing or dead. After it arrived, by your own admission, no less than three people have died, each of them with the precise same wounds on their throat as I myself bear.

SEWARD
But you don't remember what caused them.

MINA

Does that matter? Surely that coincidence is too extreme to be taken as merely that.

SEWARD

I would be far more comfortable were there more evidence of some tangible nature.

JONATHAN

My wish is the opposite. I long to be mistaken. But the Holy Sisters and all those in the nearby village remain convinced that Dracula would desecrate the bodies of their recently departed.

MINA

They must have some reason to fear such a thing.

SEWARD

Superstition.

[Enter Quincey. FX: Door opens and closes.]

QUINCEY

Art is not yet snoring, but close. So, are we doing this or not?

SEWARD

Is this something you support?

QUINCEY

Better to be safe, Jack. Besides, just checking that Lucy is still there isn't going to cause her any harm. Getting to stop thinking about that idea is worth it to me.

SEWARD

I cannot agree. Nor can I condone violating anyone's grave, much less that of..., well, because of a set of superstitions accepted as gospel a thousand miles from here!

JONATHAN

My apologies. I did not mean to suggest we should open Lucy's grave.

SEWARD

No?

MINA

Not at all.

JONATHAN

I believe we should examine her tomb and insure no other has been there, no other has entered it. Even stand guard if need be.

QUINCEY

You said it yourself, Jack—no way she died of natural causes.

SEWARD

[After a deep pause]
Very well. To hold vigil, then. I may endorse that. Yes.

QUINCEY

Here then.

[FX: A pistol is drawn out from a holster.]

No offense, Harker, but you don't look the type to know how to use one of these.

JONATHAN

Correct.

QUINCEY

[Handing Seward a pistol.]
But I know Jack does.

SEWARD

It has been a few years. But I recall the basics well enough. Should the necessity arise, then.

QUINCEY

I need to stay here, watch over Art.

MINA

We should have thought to hire a servant or two, some one to stay the night.

SEWARD

You minds have been on other matters.

MINA

Yes. Please excuse me while I get a coat.

SEWARD

A coat? I'm sorry.

JONATHAN

Yes. Her coat.

SEWARD

You don't mean—you intend to come with us? Mr. Harker?

MINA

We will face what comes, together.

JONATHAN

For better and for worse.

SEWARD

This strikes me as unwise, but I shall not argue.

QUINCEY
Don't think it would do any good if you did, Jack.

> *[FX: The sounds of the parlor fade
> away.]*

Scene 13

> *[The graveyard not far from the sea,
> later that nigh. Enter Kate Reed. FX:
> Winds, the sound of distant surf, maybe
> the cry of owls or ravens.]*

KATE REED
Of course, I forgive you. That is what friends do. You forgive me. I forgive
you. But..wait...you said to go home. Home. Where is that? My home?
Where else should I go but...here? Yes. I'll wait for you. Home.

> *[FX: The opening of a creaking, old
> door to a crypt. Footsteps approach.
> Enter Mina, Seward, Jonathan, their
> voices growing louder as they
> approach.]*

MINA
Of course we must look inside.

SEWARD
That is not what I agreed upon.

MINA
I have the key.

SEWARD
No doubt, but we are not violators of a grave. Or are we?

JONATHAN
Not. We are guardians. We look for evidence of a grave un-disturbed.

MINA
Un-disturbed, un-touched. Exactly as we last saw it.

SEWARD
And what have you in that bag, Mr. Harker?

JONATHAN
A variety of tools, most, if not all, useless. I hope. Also, a flask of brandy I
feel certain we will all appreciate before long.

SEWARD
You are governed by your fears, Mr. Harker.

JONATHAN

Among other things.

MINA

The door. Open.

SEWARD

Oh bloody hell! My apologies, Mrs. Harker.

MINA

Damn damn damn damn! I was hoping...

JONATHAN

I, as well.

MINA

Come! We have to see.

SEWARD

Wait! Surely there is no need for haste!

[FX: Creaking of the door again.]

KATE REED

Go away. All of you.

SEWARD

God in heaven.

KATE REED

Go! Now! You don't belong here! None of you! Especially you.

MINA

Why me in particular?

KATE REED

Get away from here!

SEWARD

Miss Reed! Look at me. I say, look at me this instant!

KATE REED

Doctor...Seward? Sir?

SEWARD

Miss Reed, I must insist you tell me what you are doing here?

KATE REED

Why I am here?

SEWARD

Precisely that. Miss Reid, do you yourself know?

KATE REID

I am here because she told me...she told me...I am waiting...I...

[FX: A body falling to the ground in a faint.]

SEWARD

Dear God.

MINA

Do you know her, Doctor?

SEWARD

She's an Attendant at my sanitorium, was close to one of the patients I mentioned earlier. And yes, you see? Here on her throat?

MINA

The same wounds!

SEWARD

Exactly. She's still alive, fortunately. Just in shock, and I suspect, exhaustion. Her name is Kate Reed. Do you know her?

MINA

No.

SEWARD

She said something once about knowing Lucy, or having known her. Harker! What are you doing?

JONATHAN

[From a distance]
This young woman was inside Lucy's tomb.

MINA

What do you see?

JONATHAN

Nothing much. The wreath we left has been disturbed.

SEWARD

Yes, that is upsetting, but--I have a patient here who needs attention this very second. I shall need help to carry her back the carriage, and then, to shelter. The sanitorium is close enough.

JONATHAN

We need to know what happened.

SEWARD

We need to save this young woman's life!

MINA

I shall stay.

JONATHAN

No!

SEWARD

Stay? Why the Devil does anyone need to stay?

MINA

You need to help Dr. Seward. Leave me the bag and all the tools. Hurry back to me.

SEWARD

I knew it. The pair of you are keeping something from me. But never mind that. I cannot carry Miss Reed by myself as far as the carriage. You, Harker, you needs must help. Now.

JONATHAN

Very well. Mina--

MINA

I know, my love.

JONATHAN

Here.

[FX: Movement of the bag.]

MINA

I remember everything you told me.

SEWARD

Are you coming or not?

JONATHAN

Yes. I am.

[FX: Sounds of the wind and surf fade away.]

Scene 14

[Parlor at Hillingham House. Enter Arthur. FX: The sound of a that room's clock. Door opens.]

ARTHUR

Bloody hell. Not drunk enough. Where's the damn brandy?

[Enter LucyFX: Door opens. The vampire sound.]

Quince? That you? I need more to drink.

LUCY

He is asleep my love.

ARTHUR

I'm having a dream.

LUCY

Do you like my outfit? It belongs to Jonathan but he won't mind. I've always wanted to try dressing up like a man.

ARTHUR

Beautiful. So beautiful.

LUCY

Thank you. I've always thought the same of you.

ARTHUR

I should not have waited. Too late.

LUCY

Not too late, my love. Kiss me now. Caress me now. Here, in this dream.

ARTHUR

You look...amazing.

LUCY

Let me kiss you, my love. You need not even stand.

ARTHUR

I love you.

LUCY

You can call me Quincey if you like.

ARTHUR

I...I...

LUCY

Shhhhhh.

> *[FX: The sound of a bite, as if into a soft apple, as Arthur sighs in pain and pleasure. The ticking of the clock, Arthur's sighs, the vampire sound all fade.]*

Scene 15

> *[Seward's office, later. Seward and Kate Reed discovered. FX: The familiar clock of this office.]*

KATE REED

Dr. Seward sir?

SEWARD

Yes? Do you want to say something?

KATE REED

Where am I? Is this your office?

SEWARD

Yes. Just for now. We're preparing a bed for you in one of the private rooms.

KATE REED

But--

SEWARD

We—that is, myself and some others—found you bleeding in the graveyard on the cliffs.

KATE REED

Bleeding?

SEWARD

Nothing serious. But you have a pair of wounds on your throat. Do you remember how you got them?

KATE REED

No, sir. I remember...it is odd.

SEWARD

Tell me.

KATE REED

I went to pay my respects to Miss Westenra.

SEWARD

You told me you knew her.

KATE REED

In school. Years and years ago. Her father was dead, her mother dying. My mother was dead, my father about to join her. No brothers. No sisters, either of us. We were clever. And lonely. *[She goes silent.]*

SEWARD

And? Miss Reed?

KATE REED

I thought I saw her. Just walking out of the fog, white as milk except for her eyes. They looked like tiny red stars. She apologized. Then hugged me. But, that is not possible, is it? I must have been coming down with a fever or something!

SEWARD

That is precisely what I suspect. Body and soul, the one from fever, the other from mourning. You had, as it were, a waking dream before you fainted. Good thing I and my friends found you. We also were paying respects to Lucy.

KATE REED

That's good. Nice to know she didn't end like poor Miss Renfield. All alone.

SEWARD

Miss Renfield was not alone. She had you and she had me. Neither are you alone. Do you have any family I should contact?

KATE REED

No, sir.

SEWARD

Well. You are still not alone. I have an important errand, but shall check in upon you later. We shall visit, and we shall talk. Share things. And you will grow stronger. I promise.

KATE REED

Thank you, sir.

SEWARD

Now, Miss Cotswald will come and take you to your room. Alas, I must seek out my friends immediately. But, as I promise, we shall talk later. After you have had a chance to sleep. Good night, Miss Reed.

> *[FX: Door opens and closes. As it does, the distinctive sound of Seward's clock stops.]*

Scene 16

> *[The Westenra tomb. Mina enters. FX: Winds from the outside. Also tools at work, tight screws being slowly unwound from wood. Mina's breathing indicates effort.]*

MINA

I pray you are here, Lucy. I pray my Jonathan is wrong. Please let us be wrong.

> *[FX: Another screw makes its way out of the coffin. It falls to the stone floor, creating a small pinging echo.]*

Two more to go.

> *[FX: Footsteps approach. Mina' reaches into her bag and pulls out a revolver. She cocks the hammer. The footsteps get louder. Enter Jonathan.]*

Jonathan! Thank heavens.

JONATHAN

No revolver would work against Dracula, my love.

MINA

I have the relic in my pocket should all else fail. However, I feared the Count might have minions, as you described.

JONATHAN

Here, you stand guard while I finish with the screws.

MINA

Where is Jack?

[FX: As Jonathan speaks, the same mechanical sounds of a screw being removed.]

JONATHAN

Looking after that young woman. I fear her presence means this coffin must be empty.

MINA

If so, how did Lucy escape from it? Look how much effort it is taking us, and we have tools, approaching the task from the outside.

[FX: Again an echoing ping as a screw falls to the tomb floor. Once more, effort begins on removing the last from the coffin.]

JONATHAN

But these matters are not natural. The laws of nature don't to have the same impact. Half the legends contradict each other. But a few things are consistent, no matter what the source. Those wounds for one. The way these things avoid sunlight. They never desecrate churches and saints can banish them.

MINA

You said they have to return to their graves during the day.

JONATHAN

Every single source says that.

MINA

But Dracula's grave must be hundreds and hundreds of miles away.

[FX: The final screw falls with a ping onto the stone floor of the tomb.]

So how can Dracula be here, in Whitby? He...oh. Oh! The boxes of earth on the *Demeter*! Jonathan—he moved his grave! His entire grave.

[FX: Another set of footsteps approach, growing closer. After a few moments they enter the tomb. Enter Seward.]

SEWARD

An explanation is called for. Immediately.

MINA

Jack—we need to know. Not believe, not hope, not fear. Know.

SEWARD

Know what?

JONATHAN

That Lucy remains here. Undisturbed.

SEWARD

By anyone save yourselves.

MINA

The wounds, Dr. Seward. Those on Miss...Reed, you said? Are they the same as on Lucy, and on two of your patients, and on Jonathan?

SEWARD

Identical. And?

JONATHAN

Let us make sure. If Lucy is still here, then we can all feel relief, reseal her casket and go home. That is what we all desire. For more reasons than you know.

SEWARD

You suspect something, a specific thing. I don't know what it is, and you won't say.

MINA

Let us prove ourselves wrong.

SEWARD

How?

JONATHAN

We take the lid off Lucy's casket.

MINA

To see if she is still there.

SEWARD

As opposed to? *[Silence.]*

JONATHAN

We are doing what we must.

SEWARD

You are the pair of you, insane.

[FX: Steps on the stone tomb floor, and grunts as casket lid is lifted off then put

to the side.]

MINA

Thank god!

JONATHAN

She must have been a coincidence, that young woman we found.

MINA

Dr. Seward. Our fears are proven wrong. Now, we shall put the lid of her casket back, and fasten it anew. Let her rest in eternal peace. I said a moment ago "Thank God" and I say that again with all my heart. Thank God Almighty. *[A beat]* What's wrong?

SEWARD

She's breathing.

JONATHAN

Show me.

SEWARD

It is very slight, but look carefully at the nostrils, and the chest. Movement.

JONATHAN

I don't see it.

SEWARD

But I do.

[Enter Lucy. FX: The vampire sound.]

More, I know beyond any shred of the slightest doubt she exhibited nothing of the kind before... before. Frankly it beggars the imagination that anyone sealed in that wooden box for over a day and night could still be able to breathe. This is not possible!

MINA

Oh, no.

SEWARD

What? Oh my god!

LUCY

All of you here? Shall all my friends appear to me like this?

SEWARD

But you're there...in your grave!

LUCY

I suppose so. Oh Jack, I hurt you so much. Would I had known better, been wiser. My hero.

SEWARD

Get away from me!

LUCY

Am I so changed in your eyes?

SEWARD

Your eyes burn, just like red stars! Your mouth—there's blood there! Fresh, wet blood.

LUCY

I am what I am Jack. And I love you. The past is the past. It matters nothing. Come to me, my gallant Jack.

MINA

Lucy!

LUCY

Mina? Wait, what is that? It burns! It hurts to look at. Put it away.

MINA

I won't let you hurt him.

LUCY

Put it away! It hurts.

MINA

I am sorry, Lucy. More than I have words to say. But, no.

SEWARD

Harker, what are you doing?

JONATHAN

What I hoped I wouldn't have to. A stake of hawthorn wood.

> *[FX: A hammer coming down hard on a wooden stake, driving the latter into something with consistency of flesh. With each strike of the hammer, Lucy gasps. After a few strong blows, the pounding stops.]*

LUCY

What is this?

SEWARD

Harker! For the love of God!

LUCY

Where are you going? Where are all of you going? Come back! Don't leave!

> *[FX: The vampire sound fades away.]*

MINA

Rest in peace, dear one.

SEWARD

She...she vanished. To where? What have you done?

MINA

She has gone to God, Dr. Seward. The Devil holds her in thrall no more.

> *[FX: The winds continue for a few moments. Jonathan drops the hammer which echoes as it strikes the stone floor. In the distance, the sound of seagulls begin. Then all sounds fade.]*

Scene 17

> *[Hillingham House, later that day. Enter Mina, Quincey, Jonathan. FX: Distinctive sound of the parlor's clock. Door opens then closes. Enter Seward.]*

QUINCEY

How is he, Jack?

SEWARD

Unconscious. Weak. Rest and time, a good diet will heal his body pretty much completely.

JONATHAN

And his mind?

SEWARD

Time, not I, can tell that. We shall have to see. Right now, I cannot even tell how much he remembers. Hope nobody minds if I have a drink. Early, I know, but...

MINA

Of course. Please.

SEWARD

Anyone else care to join me?

QUINCEY

Not yet.

JONATHAN

No, thank you.

MINA

Not for me. You go ahead.

> *[Silence for a moment.]*

QUINCEY

Jack?

SEWARD

Changed my mind. Want to keep as clear a head as I can manage.

QUINCEY

Good.

SEWARD

So, I presume Mr. Harker you remember far more than you admitted about your time in this Castle Dracula.

JONATHAN

Not that much more. I recall Dracula sinking his fangs into my throat more than once, leaving me weak as a fresh-born kitten. He talked a lot. But it wasn't a straightforward, or anything like a conversation most of the time. Asked me what I saw when I looked at the room we were in. He wanted to know if I saw the tapestries. There weren't any. Then he said something about boxes, fifty boxes his servants were shipping all the way to Varna for transport to England. He kept wondering out loud why he was going.

MINA

We think we know why he needed those boxes.

QUINCEY

The ones on the Demeter? Manifest said they were filled with clay.

MINA

His grave. He must return to his grave during the day. Those boxes of earth— they are his grave. He moved it.

SEWARD

There isn't a person in England who wouldn't call what you just said totally mad. Not a sane one,
 anyway.

JONATHAN

Then we are all mad. With identical madness, all of us. Even to the point of seeing the same hallucinations.

SEWARD

I know.

QUINCEY

If Dracula is asleep right now, he'll find out what we did tonight. How powerful will he be then? I mean, from what you say he easily manhandled you, Harker. Somehow hid on board ship for four weeks. None of us or anyone else saw him enter either Hillingham or Jack's sanitorium. What weapons work against him? That relic of Jack's, you said did the trick?

MINA

From what I've read every Church in Romania contains a tiny relic of a saint. These creatures never enter there.

QUINCEY

Do we have any more? Jack?

SEWARD

I do not.

JONATHAN

If we do not act today, he can move his boxes of earth. He will move them.
God knows where.

SEWARD

Can you cut his head off?

JONATHAN

According to legend.

MINA

Why?

SEWARD

I still have my sword.

QUINCEY

Can you shoot them?

MINA

Legends don't say anything about guns.

QUINCEY

Guess we'll find out, then.

SEWARD

I'll need to go get my sword. And check on Miss Reed.

MINA

How is she?

SEWARD

Much the same as Arthur. If they remain unmolested both should make a full
recovery.

JONATHAN

We dare not waste more time.

MINA

No. We will all need lanterns.

QUINCEY

And revolvers. Just in case. And you, Miss Mina, you keep that relic on your
person.

> *[FX: The sound of the clock stops
> abuptly.]*

Scene 18

*[Inside the ruined manor of Carfax,
later. FX: Winds through broken
walls. The sound of rats scurrying on
the floor, which soon fades. The
turning of a key, then the swinging
open of an old door. Enter Jonathan,
Mina, Quincey, Seward.]*

QUINCEY

Harker. Is this what Castle Dracula was like?

JONATHAN

Same smell.

SEWARD

Like the sick room. Or a morgue.

QUINCEY

Well, here's a bit of good news. Look at the floor.

SEWARD

The dust.

JONATHAN

The men who delivered the boxes here said they put them in the crypts.

QUINCEY

And here is their path, a trail in the dust. All we have to do is follow it.

MINA

Let us begin.

*[FX: Steps go forward, then fade. The
vampire sound rises, then the flapping
of vast wings. Both wings and vampire
sound fade. Steps return.]*

QUINCEY

Damn. Something has been turning up this dust. The trail is gone.

JONATHAN

The boxes were not small. We can safely dismiss all the smaller corridors I
think. This main
hallway seems to run the length of the structure. The crypts must be along it.

SEWARD

Didn't they give some kind of better directions?

JONATHAN

I didn't speak with them directly. They were working elsewhere so Mr.
Hawkins repeated what they told him.

MINA

We should have waited, learned more. Too late, now. Even if we leave, he will know we were here.

JONATHAN

Shine all your lamps that way. [*Beat or two.*] That is a door is it not? Quite large and wide open.

SEWARD

And a stone angel on either side. Looks like a crypt to me. Or at least it could be.

[FX: Echoing steps as they proceed.
After several moments they stop.]

JONATHAN

Here they are.

SEWARD

Fifty you said?

JONATHAN

Yes.

SEWARD

Too dark. I cannot count.

QUINCEY

This place is full of candles. I'll start lighting them.

[FX: A matching being struck.]

JONATHAN

We don't know. One should be his coffin.

SEWARD

They all look like coffins. More or less. I count twenty against this wall. Harker?

[FX: The vampire sound. Enter
Dracula.]

JONATHAN

Fifteen here.

QUINCEY

These candles must have been left here by the men who delivered the boxes.

DRACULA

Some. Others have waited here years, and years. Harker? You escaped. Made your way home. I am impressed. Are you why I came here? No one has invaded my sanctuary in what feels like many long lifetimes.

[FX: A series of loud gunshots echo in

*room, as Quincey empties his guns into
Dracula.]*

QUINCEY

Damn!

DRACULA

Interesting. Like tiny cannons. You show skill in their use. *[A beat.]* I know
you. In a way. I was you.

QUINCEY

Guns don't work. I'll bet knives will.

DRACULA

I walked in danger, and by becoming dangerous thought that would protect me.
Like you, I was wrong.

*[FX: The sound of a scuffle, albeit a
short one. The sound of a knife falling
to the stone floor.]*

One day, Slayer of Men, you and I shall talk of killing, of how it made us feel
and what we thought we accomplished. Maybe then, we will know the
answers. When we have both crossed into the shadows.

QUINCEY

You first.

DRACULA

No.

*[FX: The crunch of a neck being
crushed and/or snapped. A body falls
to the floor with a heavy thud.]*

SEWARD

Quince!

DRACULA

Are you Doctor Jack? I have heard of you. Lucy spoke of you. With great
affection. I will be a little sorry to kill you. You as well, Harker.

MINA

Dracula!

*[FX: The vampire sound falters
somehow, and Dracula gasps in
surprise and some pain.]*

DRACULA

What is that?

SEWARD

A holy relic.

DRACULA

You three are wise. Wiser than many far older. Oh, Harker, I am so impressed.

MINA

Jonathan! Dr. Seward. Look here! See!

JONATHAN

My god.

SEWARD

His coffin!

DRACULA

I have felt pain again, here. And tasted fear, even a little bit of hope. Now— surprise. This is wonderful. But I do not think you can open my coffin. It was sealed in resins and as you can see, fastened with iron bands.

JONATHAN

He's right.

SEWARD

No! Look at it, there are cracks all along the wood!

DRACULA

You have accomplished much, though. Please, be proud.

MINA

He shall be proud. We all will.

DRACULA

Is this your fiancee, Harker? Or by now, wife? How extremely brave.

JONATHAN

You stand back!

DRACULA

I do not take orders. Not even from those I admire. Not when I was a man, nor now, when I am so much more, and less. And even now, you have not defeated me. Still, I am most impressed with you all.

[FX: The distant sound of many, many tiny animals approaching.]

JONATHAN

What is that sound?

SEWARD

Rats.

DRACULA

In their hundreds. Your relic will have no impact upon them.

[FX: Footsteps.]

SEWARD

They're coming down the hall.

> *[FX: Grunts as he tries to shut the
> door, unsuccessfully. The sound of the
> rats steadily grow closer.]*

The damn door won't budge!

MINA

Count Dracula!

DRACULA

Yes, beloved of Harker? What is your name?

MINA

Mina. And if I am brave, also am I wise. The tears of Saint Veronica. Here in
this bottle. It holds you a bay does it not? But what if I open this bottle, thus?
And then, pour its contents through one of these cracks onto whatever is left of
your bones? Worth finding out!

JONATHAN

Can we shoot them?

SEWARD

Nowhere near enough bullets. Wait, I have an idea!

> *[FX: The sound of a small amount of
> liquid poured out onto some surface.
> Dracula gasps, and the vampire sound
> falters.]*

JONATHAN

Dear God.

DRACULA

Now I know. Why I came here. The shadows finally beckon to me.

SEWARD

Harker! Open your lamp and throw it at the rats!

DRACULA

I feel...I...have not the words. Memories returning to me. Voices.

> *[FX: Jonathan throws the lamp, which
> breaks, ignites the kerosene and dust,
> making the rats scream and flee. The
> sound of flames steadily increases.]*

MINA

He's aging.

DRACULA
[Weaker and weaker]
Far too many to count. Men and children and women. My heart—it beats
again! And begins to fail. Bones. Flesh. Ashes become ashes. Dust returns to
dust.

MINA
The fire.

JONATHAN
Yes. We need to flee at once.

DRACULA
I had forgotten what it felt like, to die.

SEWARD
I brought a sword. Let me remind you.

DRACULA
Who better has the right? Your are a healer are you not?

> *[FX: The slash of a sword, cutting off*
> *Dracula's head. An echoing*
> *moan/scream rises then fades as the*
> *vampire sound fades away, replaced by*
> *the sound of ever rising flames, and*
> *three sets of footsteps fleeing, all of*
> *which which fades. Silence.]*

Scene 19

> *[Seward's office. Day. FX: The*
> *muffled sounds of Whitby harbor*
> *through the window. The apparatus of*
> *Seward's phonograph being set up.*
> *When Seward speaks it sounds as if he*
> *speaks into a funnel.]*

SEWARD
I never thought to use this device again. It has been a one year. Arthur left
Whitby as soon as he physically could. I wish him well. Mr. and Mrs. Harker
now have a son. Carfax remains a burned out ruin. I try not to think on it. But
today, a strong and kind woman has agreed to become my wife. Life is brief,
full of woe, sickness, and oblivion. But there is work. And happiness. And
love. For a time. I think that may be enough. Or can be. Miss Reed, that is,
Kate, she understands. Perhaps as none other. We shall face what comes,
together.

> *[FX: Sounds fade.]*

CURTAIN

ABOUT THE AUTHOR

David MacDowell Blue, born in San Francisco, raised in Florida, schooled in New York City, now resides in Los Angeles. He has a BA in Theatre Arts and graduated from the National Shakespeare Conservatory. Since 2012 he has been a theatre reviewer online, and currently belongs to Fierce Backbone Theatre Company in Los Angeles. Previous plays include *Carmilla*, *After the Lighthouse Fell*, *Shadows on the Air*, and *Moonlight Preludes*. He firmly believes live theatre cannot compete with film and television for naturalistic recreation and should not try. Rather theatre should embrace masks and rituals, stirring the audience's imagination, and its existence in three-dimensional space.

His website is www.davidmacdowellblue.com

Printed in Great Britain
by Amazon

62495994R00052